DIRTY WEEKEND

A J.J. Graves Mystery

LILIANA HART

ALSO BY LILIANA HART

JJ Graves Mystery Series

Dirty Little Secrets

A Dirty Shame

Dirty Rotten Scoundrel

Down and Dirty

Dirty Deeds

Dirty Laundry

Dirty Money

A Dirty Job

Dirty Devil

Playing Dirty

Dirty Martini

Dirty Dozen

Dirty Minds

Addison Holmes Mystery Series

Whiskey Rebellion

Whiskey Sour

Whiskey For Breakfast

Whiskey, You're The Devil

Whiskey on the Rocks

Whiskey Tango Foxtrot

Whiskey and Gunpowder

Whiskey Lullaby

The Scarlet Chronicles

Bouncing Betty

Hand Grenade Helen

Front Line Francis

The Harley and Davidson Mystery Series

The Farmer's Slaughter

A Tisket a Casket

I Saw Mommy Killing Santa Claus

Get Your Murder Running

Deceased and Desist

Malice in Wonderland

Tequila Mockingbird

Gone With the Sin

Grime and Punishment

Blazing Rattles

A Salt and Battery

Curl Up and Dye

First Comes Death Then Comes Marriage

Box Set 1

Box Set 2

Box Set 3

The Gravediggers

The Darkest Corner

Gone to Dust

Say No More

To Scott—I love you.

Three things cannot long be hidden: the sun, the moon, and the truth.

~Confucius

Everyone is a moon, and has a dark side which he never shows to anybody.

~Mark Twain

CHAPTER ONE

I PICKED UP THE PACE AS AN URGENT BREEZE pushed me from behind. Fresh leaves rustled overhead and gray clouds covered the sun, setting a monochrome filter over Bloody Mary. It was par for the course. Virginia was experiencing one of the wettest springs on record.

I'd left my umbrella at the funeral home, so I hurried my steps down Catherine of Aragon, hoping the towering oaks that lined the streets would give me cover as I made my way downtown. I'd at least had the foresight to put on my black parka as I'd let myself out the back door.

My name is J.J. Graves and there was peace in the monotony of routine. For the last several months I'd decided getting fresh air and exercise might be good for me, so I'd gotten into the habit of arriving at the funeral home early and walking to the Towne Square for my morning coffee. It wasn't a hardship. Jack said I made terrible coffee. My coffee kept me awake and functional, especially during my residency at the hospital, so I'd learned to endure.

The fact that I usually bought a donut to go with my coffee probably balanced out the calories I worked off on my walk. I'm a stress eater, so I don't really have an excuse. I'm just fortunate I still have my metabolism, but I hear that will disappear by the time I'm forty and all those donuts will catch up to me.

You might be wondering why I'm stress eating. It's an easy enough answer. It's also the same reason I decided that exercise and fresh air might be good for me. Jack and I have been trying to have a baby for the past six months or so. So far, we haven't had any luck, though we've had loads of practice.

I'm a doctor, so I know how these things work. It's too soon to be worried about why I'm not pregnant yet, and there could be any number of sound medical reasons. I tend to lean toward the idea that my stress is caused by my career choices. If the things I've seen in life affect my mind and body in strange ways, I figure my reproductive system has its own kind of PTSD to deal with and it's just trying to figure out what normal is. The rest of me was still trying to figure out what normal was too.

The funeral home was my day job. I was fourth-generation mortician, and Graves Funeral Home was finally running in the black and on the right side of the law. My family would probably be devastated to know this, but they're too busy hauling coal in hell to care too much.

I used to say that being a mortician was in my blood, but since I found out that the family I'd thought were mine were nothing more than frauds, con artists, and criminals—not to mention kidnappers since they'd taken me from my birth mother—I don't feel the familial guilt I once did for not willingly taking over the reins of my inheritance.

Running a funeral home is like most jobs, I imagine. There's a lot of organization and customer service involved. We provide a service of dignity and respect. With the added touch of pumping people's loved ones full of embalming fluid, cremating them in a fiery furnace, or burying them six feet under. It was an irony that didn't go unnoticed.

I'd grown the business to the point where I didn't have to be as hands on as I once had. I was kind of like a death CPA. I had a bunch of interns and staff who did most of the grimy work, and my signature went on everything because the government likes to have someone to blame and tax.

Along with the funeral home, I was also the coroner for King George County, which occupied most of the other hours of my day. The upside to this was that I got to work alongside Jack. The downside was we lived and breathed the job, and we typically saw the worst humanity had to offer. People were generally good, and we tried to remember that. But when you put them in situations like murder investigations there was a basic instinct that crept from the depths of the soul for self-preservation. We always assume everyone is lying in a murder investigation. It made our jobs easier. It didn't translate so well though when we were off the job.

The least stressful part of either of my jobs was working with the dead. The dead never disappointed, they were always consistent, and they never talked back. It was the living that made things challenging. Plus, there was the stress I put on myself. Like worrying about why I still wasn't pregnant. It was a never-ending cycle of pressure.

I picked up the pace and waved to the driver of a blue sedan as I crossed the intersection and headed toward the Towne Square. I passed newly renovated condos and walked under a scaffold of another historic building that would end up being a homemade soap or boba tea shop. King George County was becoming another Charleston or Savannah, with its trendy shops and rising real estate costs.

But the citizens of King George were fighters and they didn't give up their land lightly. The area might be growing and new businesses and families moving in, but it wasn't big box corporations and billionaire developers. And it wasn't federal agencies from DC encroaching and trying to take what wasn't theirs. We knew these attempts were happening for a fact because our friend Carver had discovered things he wasn't supposed to know while working for the FBI. Now he was a man on the run and we hadn't heard from him in months.

"Morning, Doc," Officer Cheek said as he headed to his patrol car. He was fresh faced and spit and polished in his uniform for the start of his shift, and he held a to-go cup of coffee and a bag of donuts from Lady Jane's.

"Morning, Cheek," I said, and then I tortured myself as I passed by Lady Jane's and inhaled the most incredible aromas of powdered sugar and fried dough.

I told myself it was the line out the door that had me walking past Lady Jane's, but that was a lie. I would have stood in line for hours to taste those sweet confections and the best coffee on this side of the Atlantic. It was only a deep loyalty and friendship that had me walking past Lady Jane's and continuing across the square to the Donut Palace.

My receptionist, Emmy Lu, had been dating Tom Daly for the good part of a year now. I'd gone to kindergarten with Tom and he was a great guy, but he probably would've had more success opening a butcher shop or a bar. Tom was a guy's guy, and he was as basic as they came. He was meat and potatoes. He was a plain glazed donut. But he was solid and stable, and what he didn't make in donut income he made up for as a handyman.

All these things were important because Emmy Lu loved him, and she had five boys to raise since her no-good ex-husband left her high and dry. But the Donut Palace had been a staple the last twenty-five years, run by Tom's father before he passed, and Emmy Lu worked there for extra money four days a week. I wasn't sure how Tom could afford to pay her, but that probably had more to do with hormones than best business practices. The last thing I wanted was for

Tom and Emmy Lu to be in a financial fix, so I passed by Lady Jane's every morning and walked straight to the Donut Palace, where there was no line out the door and plenty of donuts on the shelf.

"Morning," I said, as the little bell tinkled above the door.

"Morning, Jaye," Emmy Lu said from behind the counter. She was a short, plump woman with a kind face and dimples. If I had to think of Suzy Homemaker, Emmy Lu is who'd come to mind. She wore a white apron over a waist that had been thickened by five pregnancies and donuts, and her fluffy brown hair was piled on top of her head in a messy bun.

"I was wondering if you were going to make it in this morning," she said. "It's looking nasty out there."

On the mornings Emmy Lu worked at the Donut Palace, she opened with Tom at four and then she'd stay and work the counter until she had to be at the funeral home at nine. I didn't know where she found the energy to work two jobs and raise five boys, but if I was a betting woman, I'd bet that Emmy Lu could probably rule the world and still make cookies at the end of the day.

"Forecast says there's no end in sight," I said.

"We've got two graveside services this weekend, and six-foot holes that are going to be full of muddy water. The last two days were a reprieve. I'm hoping the excavator can get into the cemetery and get those holes dug this morning without getting stuck. I tried to talk the families out of doing a graveside service and using the funeral home instead, but people get ideas in their heads of how they want things to be and there's no convincing them otherwise."

Emmy Lu clicked her tongue in sympathy. "I don't know why people insist on a graveside service when they know good and well the weather here is as fickle as Norma Greenbough's dating life since her husband died."

I grunted in agreement.

"Norma's all over the place," Emmy Lu said. "Signing up for a Tinder account one minute and then after she swipes right she's beating the men off with a stick and telling them she's not interested. No one wants to see a woman her age on Tinder."

I hmmed and let out a quiet sigh of disappointment as I looked into the donut case. There were no bear claws or apple fritters. No cream- or jelly-filled donuts. It was just glazed and chocolate and what looked like a sad blueberry cake donut on the bottom shelf.

"People grieve in different ways," I said.

Emmy Lu snorted and bent over the case to put two chocolate donuts in a bag. "She's not grieving if you ask me. I think she's feeling guilty. Jimmy Martin is the manager over at Stromboli's and I heard it straight from his lips that Norma was berating Richard up one side and down the other because he forgot their anniversary. Jimmy said Richard looked straight at Norma, told her to shut up, and then fell face-first in his tiramisu. Didn't even get to finish it first before he died."

I grinned and poured coffee from a carafe into an insulated cup and was liberal with the cream and sugar to ease the bitterness.

"The pool of potential male candidates on Tinder in King George can't be many," I said. "Norma will run out of choices eventually. In the meantime, we've got Bruce Lichner and Merilee Walling to bury in a watery grave this weekend. And all their friends and family can stand grave-side and be miserable with them."

Emmy Lu shivered. "Fifty dollars says there's twice as many people who show up after the service for the casseroles and dessert bar."

"That's a sucker's bet," I said.

Tom poked his head from around back and said, "Morning, J.J. Just pulling a fresh batch from the ovens. You got here just in time before the rush."

Emmy Lu met my eyes and her brows rose to her hairline, but she didn't say anything. She didn't have to. Everything she was thinking was written right across her face. Emmy Lu was a terrible poker player.

"Take your time coming in this morning," I told her. "The schedule is clear until this afternoon when we have to start prepping for viewings."

Emmy Lu clucked her tongue and said, "If you ask me, digging watery graves is going to be the least of our problems this weekend. It's Friday the thirteenth and a full moon."

I shuddered and said, "I hate full moons. I thought it was bad when I worked at the hospital, but I had some of my most interesting patients show up when there was a full moon. Like the guy who accidentally shot himself in the head with his nail gun."

Emmy Lu snickered and bit into her own donut.

"Drove himself to the hospital and was sitting in the waiting room bold as you please next to a kid who'd broken his arm jumping off his roof and into a swimming pool. But full moons are a whole different animal now that I'm the coroner.

Generally full moon bad decisions end with a body bag instead of an nail extraction and a cast."

"Well, good luck," Emmy Lu said. "I'll either see you at the office this afternoon or sometime next week."

I paid and said my goodbyes, having every intention of heading over to the sheriff's office to see if I could bum a Lady Jane's donut from the breakroom, but my phone rang before I could step foot in that direction.

"Graves," I said, recognizing the number from dispatch.

"You've got a body at 1822 Monastery Court in Bloody Mary," Barbara Blanton said. "Sheriff is already on scene and requesting the coroner."

"I'm about ten minutes out," I said and disconnected before I got stuck on the phone with Barbara. If you wanted to know anything about anyone, Barbara was the person to see. Most of the time it was the truth too.

I looked up at the sky again and swore under my breath as a low rumble of thunder vibrated the air around me. I took back my earlier sentiment about there being peace in routine. If I'd had the sense that God gave a goose I'd have taken one look at the sky and driven in my car to get donuts and coffee. That same goose sense probably would have taken me straight to Lady Jane's instead of clear across the other side of the Towne Square.

"You okay, Doc?" asked a familiar voice.

A patrol car had pulled right in front of me and I'd been so busy condemning my bad decisions that I hadn't even noticed. Officer Chen sat behind the wheel of her black-and-white and the look on her face made me wonder how long she'd been trying to get my attention.

"I'm fine," I said. "Just regretting some life choices."

She looked at the Donut Palace coffee and bag of donuts in my hand and nodded sympathetically. "We've all been there."

"I just got the call for the body pickup on Monastery Court," I said. "My car is at the funeral home."

"Oh," she said, realizing I'd been full of a myriad of bad life choices that morning. "Hop in. I can swing you by. I heard it was a real doozy."

"Homicide?" I asked.

"Don't know the details," she said, shrugging. "But I'd take your boots. I heard it was real messy."

"Lovely," I said.

"You should eat a donut. You're going to need some fortification." She looked at my donut bag again. "Of course, it's times like these you need real sugar. Or maybe a cream-filled."

I sighed dejectedly and said, "You're right." Then I tossed the coffee and donut bag into the nearest trash can before I got in the patrol car.

CHAPTER TWO

THE FIRST DROPS OF RAIN STARTED TO FALL JUST AS I pulled into the driveway at 1822 Monastery Court. It was in one of the older, established neighborhoods in Bloody Mary and only a few minutes from the funeral home.

The bad thing about finding a body in Bloody Mary was the chances were high I would know the person. There were fewer than three thousand people in Bloody Mary and the population had stayed fairly consistent since I was a child.

King George County was divided into four towns—Bloody Mary, Nottingham, Newcastle, and King George Proper. The towns connected at the four corners right in the middle, and that's where the Towne Square had been built almost three hundred years before. Bloody Mary was in the far quadrant and it backed up to the Potomac River and a national park. It was still mostly farmland, though big developers were trying to change that. So while the rest of King George County was growing by leaps and bounds, Bloody Mary was still fairly contained. At least for now.

Monastery Court was full of old Victorian houses that sat on a couple of acres. There were towering trees and cracks in the sidewalks from the roots. The houses in this area were hard to come by. They were usually passed on from one generation to the next. But if one of the houses did happen to slip through someone's fingers, it sold quickly and at a premium price.

There were police cars parked in front of a well-kept three-story house with gingerbread trim. It was freshly painted yellow with white trim and burgundy shutters. Despite the fresh paint, it looked as gloomy as the weather. There were ceramic pots on the porch planted with drooping hydrangeas, and the front lawn held pools of water.

Blue and red flashing lights swirled from the police cars, but there were no sirens or signs of any of their drivers. No neighbors stood on porches to see what was going on. I shivered once and zipped up my black coveralls and slipped my feet into my boots, and then I grabbed my medical bag and closed the trunk of my Suburban. I went ahead and pulled out the gurney, knowing the weather would just get worse, and I rolled it up to the big covered porch and lifted it up the stairs.

The front door opened and Jack met me at the threshold. "Thought it would take you longer to get here," he said. "I figured when you got the call you were still debating whether to eat Tom's donuts or give in and go to Lady Jane's."

I'd known Jack my whole life, and he still had the ability to take my breath away. He was my safe place. My center of stability. And I couldn't imagine my world without him in it. By the time he'd hit his freshman year in high school, he'd finally grown into his feet, as his mother used to say. He was well over six feet, though he hadn't filled out in the shoulders until his early twenties. And filled out nicely he had.

No matter what stage of life, Jack had always had movie star good looks—he was the kid everyone liked and gravitated toward. He was Mr. Popular and captain of the football team. Once he'd progressed into manhood he'd left being simply good looking behind and moved into devastatingly handsome.

I'd helped relieve him of the moniker of

perfection by giving him the thin scar that slashed through his eyebrow. No matter how he told the story, the truth was, if he hadn't been blocking home plate, my cleat never would have made contact with his face. So he really has no one to blame for his imperfection but himself. Other than that, he'd been put together by God himself.

Jack's dark hair was a little longer than he usually kept it, but only because he hadn't had time to get a haircut, and he had a few days' growth of stubble on his face. His muscles were honed from the years he'd spent on SWAT in DC. And much to my personal satisfaction, he still kept up his fitness routine.

I narrowed my eyes as I walked past him, leaving the gurney on the porch for now. "That charming smile might work on others, but be careful. I'm feeling kind of mean. I still haven't had my coffee and I threw away the donuts so Chen wouldn't judge me. I was on my way to the sheriff's office to filch some Lady Jane's from the breakroom when I got the call from dispatch."

Jack laughed and said, "We're a no-judgment operation. Especially Chen. At least not out loud. She's a silent judger."

"She wasn't silent today," I said, rolling my

eyes. I looked around and let first impressions of the house wash over me. "Nice place."

A staircase with ornate spindles was the first thing that drew the eye, followed by a massive crystal chandelier hanging overhead. Everything was very traditional in style, and the hardwood floors looked original. "You going to tell me why I'm here?"

"The emergency operator got a call this morning from Lydia Hargrove," Jack said. "Said she went to the store and when she got back she found Steve dead in his study."

"No," I said, eyes wide. "Not Coach Hargrove. He's not even that old. Poor Mrs. Hargrove."

Mrs. Hargrove had been Jack's and my first-grade teacher. And then we'd both had Coach Hargrove when we'd gotten into high school. He'd been Jack's football coach and my history teacher. Everyone knew them, and they were well loved.

"Where's the study?" I asked, dreading what was to come. It was always much harder when you knew the dead on a personal level.

"Behind the stairs," Jack said, putting his hand on my shoulder before I could move forward.

Then I remembered what Chen said about

the scene being a messy one. "What aren't you telling me?"

"I'm not telling you anything until you get a good look," Jack said. "We'll follow procedure just like we do for every unattended death."

"Oh, man," I said, dreading it even more. "Where is everyone?"

"Plank took the call," Jack said, his mouth tight. "Mrs. Hargrove was waiting on the porch when he arrived and told him where to find the study. She didn't want to go back in the house.

"Plank followed standard operating procedure and confirmed the deceased. Unfortunately, he didn't pay attention as he approached the body, so he called for backup and waited for them to arrive so he could leave and change clothes."

"Yikes," I said. "You're really selling this one. Can't wait to get in there."

Jack winced and gave me a tight smile. "Martinez and Riley responded to Plank's call and they're doing door-to-doors to see if anyone saw or heard anything. And Mrs. Hargrove is in the kitchen with Walters. We finally got her to come back inside by taking her around to the back of the house. Plank got back a few minutes ago and is helping Martinez and Riley with the neighbors."

I smelled it before we reached the study. There was a particular smell to death in general, but the scent of blood was rich and coppery and clung to the back of your throat so you could almost taste it.

There was crime scene tape across the door so no one disturbed the area, and Jack pulled down the yellow tape and then took a black umbrella that had been propped against the wall. Then he opened the door.

"You've already done a walk-through?" I asked, looking up at the ceiling.

Sometimes it took a second for the brain to catch up with what the eyes were seeing. I let the images in my periphery blur and focused on one spot for a moment, just to let myself adjust.

"I was waiting on you," Jack said. "Plank didn't touch the body, but he was almost there before he'd assessed the entire situation. Which is why he had to change clothes."

"You live and you learn," I said.

Jack opened the umbrella and we stepped inside the room. A wet plop hit the umbrella.

It was a horrible scene. Mentally compartmentalizing was the only way to stay sane. Now wasn't the time to think about Coach Hargrove the person. Now was the time to take care of the dead and piece together the story of how and why he was no longer with us.

"Wow, look at this place," I said, still not focused on the body.

It was a room full of trophies, autographed pictures, and game paraphernalia from thirty years of coaching. It was all covered in blood spatter and what I assumed was human tissue and brain matter.

Coach Hargrove sat behind a large mahogany desk in a brown leather chair. He wore a pair of tan khakis and a blue-striped polo shirt. He'd worn a similar uniform every day of school for as long as I could remember. The only difference was the Coach Hargrove sitting in the chair was entirely missing his head.

Plop.

Plop.

"Sawed-off shotgun lying to the right of the victim," Jack said once we'd moved closer. "After you take the body I'll get the techs in here to swab and confirm this is our weapon."

"I think it's safe to say this is our weapon," I said. "Sawed-offs make a heck of a mess. As exhibited by the brains all over the ceiling."

"They're also illegal in the state of Virginia," Jack said. "Not that the law has ever stopped people from carrying whatever weapon they wanted to in King George. This is a Second Amendment county. But I generally don't see high school coaches feel the need for a weapon like this."

"Maybe it's not his," I said.

"Which is a possibility we've got to look into."

Plop.

I sighed and pulled a pair of gloves from my bag, and handed another pair to Jack. "I guess it falls under my jurisdiction to gather all the pieces and try to put Humpty Dumpty back together again."

"We get the evidence. You get the body. All of it."

"Lily is going to hate me."

"You live and learn," he said, repeating my earlier sentiment.

Lily had been my intern while she'd been finishing up school, but once she'd started her doctoral studies I'd hired her on as assistant coroner. The pay was peanuts because it was a city job, but I supplemented her income when we needed extra hands at the funeral home. And it gave her great hands-on experience. I knew I'd lose her at some point to a bigger operation as she finished medical school and needed more pathology experience, but for now, I was grateful to have her.

I studied the victim with a critical eye. I'd been trained to look for the obvious. The body always told a story, whether you were alive or dead. Were you healthy or unhealthy? Did you drink? Smoke? Do drugs? Did you work at a desk or manual labor? Were you athletic? Accident prone or abused? People thought they could hide who they really were. And maybe to an extent they could to those who didn't pay attention. But the body didn't lie.

Since I'd started working with Jack, I'd learned to look at more than just the body. Jack was able to size up a scene like no one I'd ever met before. It took me a little longer, but I was getting better at it.

"He's dressed for school," I said. I noted the athletic socks and sneakers on his feet. "Just a regular Friday, and it looks like he was ready to walk out the door."

"That's how it looks," Jack agreed. "His gym bag and leather briefcase are sitting by the front door. Rain jacket and umbrella are on the coatrack."

"Routine," I said, thinking of my earlier morning walk. "Any signs of a break-in or robbery?"

"Not as of yet, but crime scene techs are on the way," he said.

"Body is still warm. Rigor hasn't set in yet. There would have been a short window of time from when his wife left until she came back. This isn't looking good, Jack. Weapon placement, blood spatter and body positioning...it screams of a self-inflicted gunshot wound."

"I know," he said. "But this is Coach. And we'll follow protocol and treat it as a homicide until you make the official ruling."

I nodded, feeling the weight of that responsibility. "Seems odd to get everything ready for a regular day, watch your wife leave for the store, and then off yourself while she's gone. He'd know she'd be the one to come back and find him. Why would he do that?"

"Questions we might never know the answer to," Jack said.

"Looks like he put the barrel under his chin, and he probably would have had to pull the trigger with his thumb. I'll take measurements once we're back at the lab. Maybe that's the reason he sawed the barrel off. So he could do this."

"Barrel under the chin is always a risk," Jack said. "I've seen more people than I'd like who try to go out that way and end up blowing their nose off or peeling back the skin from their face."

"That's probably not a statistic your average

Joe knows when deciding to commit suicide," I said. "No papers on his desk. No computer. No suicide note. Just blood spatter and tissue."

Another plop hit the umbrella and I crouched down so I could look closely at the body. "No visible signs of a struggle, but I'll know more once I can get him on the table."

I shifted the body forward slightly so I could look at his back and beneath him. "Wallet is in the back pocket." I worked my hand beneath him to pull out the wallet and handed it to Jack.

"Again, indicative of someone who's about to walk out the door," he said.

"Blood spatter and tissue are absent from the back, meaning he was sitting in this chair from start to finish. Blowback from the gun pushed the chair into the wall. There's not a whole lot more to go on." I stood back up. "Help me get him in the bag and contained so we don't lose any more of his tissue and bone fragments. I'll have Lily and Sheldon come and gather as much of the brain matter and tissue as they can."

We worked together quickly and got Coach Hargrove bagged and left him in the chair so we didn't accidentally transfer tissue or particles.

"Other than the blood and tissue," Jack said, "this is a well-kept space. Everything is in order and organized. He was always a stickler for stuff like that. He used to tell us if we couldn't be disciplined at home then we couldn't expect to be disciplined on the field. He taught us a lot about manhood."

Jack stood with his back to me as he looked around every inch of the office space. I knew this was hard on him. Harder than he could or would let on. And I knew the best thing I could do was let him talk it out in his own time and way.

There were football helmets on a display shelf for every year Coach Hargrove won a state championship, including the year Jack's team had won. It was the shrine of a man who'd had a long and successful career.

"What happened to the 2015 helmet?" he asked.

I noted the empty spot on the shelf where he pointed. The placard was there with the date and a picture of the state winning team in a small frame, but there was no helmet to match the others on the wall.

"We can ask Mrs. Hargrove," I said.

"This is going to be a hard one for the community," Jack said. "Coach Hargrove is a hero. People are going to want someone or something to blame. No matter what this looks like at the surface, we need to dot every *I* and cross every *T*. However we can bring the most closure."

his youngest son has played football for Coach Hargrove the last three years."

"I recognize the name," Jack said. "Kid's name is Derek. I've watched him play ball. He's a heck of a quarterback. He's got potential at the college level."

"That's what the dad seems to think," Martinez said.

I was used to the meandering conversation of cops. They eventually got where they were going.

"And Joe Able didn't think hearing a gunshot was worth checking out?" Jack asked.

Martinez grinned. "He said Coach gets aggravated with the squirrels eating all his bird feed, so he'll go out from time to time and blast off a shot. Must scare the hell out of those squirrels. But Able said he doesn't do it often and they hardly pay any attention to it anymore."

"A sawed-off shotgun seems overkill for a few squirrels," I said.

"A sawed-off is overkill for anyone," Martinez said.

"Lily and Sheldon are on the way to do the body retrieval." And then I paused and clarified. "Retrieval of everything."

Riley grimaced. "I'm glad it's not me. Becky hates it when I have to strip down naked on the back porch before I can come in the house. I fell in a septic tank once and she made me take my uniform off down the street and hose off in the backyard."

"You stripping down naked anywhere is a travesty for all mankind," Martinez said. "We're all surprised Becky lets you in her bed at all."

"I've heard she keeps the lights off," one of the forensic techs said from inside the room. "She's probably never seen him naked."

"Or maybe she did and that's why she keeps the lights off," Martinez said.

I stifled a chuckle, and Jack and I left them to go find the kitchen.

There were a lot of downsides to being a first responder. There was the trauma of seeing how fragile the human body is up close and personal. And also a firsthand look at the evil that permeated the souls of people—next-door neighbors, kindergarten teachers, children, parents—we'd seen it all, and we were never surprised at the culprit. Anyone who believed in world peace was living in a fantasy land. There was good and there was evil. Evil didn't just decide to become good because someone gave them the hug they never got in childhood. Not being aware of the true evil in the world was a good way to end up buried under someone's basement.

There was also the personal toll of being a

first responder. Besides the PTSD and night-mares, there was generally a common dysfunc-tion when it came to family and personal lives. There was alcoholism, broken marriages, infi-delity, anger issues and high suicide rates—all results of trauma that accumulated over years on the job.

Jack and I were an anomaly. I'd been a mess for most of my life, and still, we'd learned how to work through it for our relationship. We still had to work through things, but at least we were working. Not everyone was that lucky.

I often wondered what made certain people gravitate toward being a first responder. Gener-ally, it was because they wanted to help people. Then they got on the job and discovered that altruistic and naïve outlook was hard to hold on to. I also wondered if those same people would make the same choices knowing what they were really signing up for.

We all learned to be matter of fact about the job. It was difficult not to become cold and calloused and desensitized at the sight of tragedy. But no matter how desensitized we became, it still affected us all, and in different ways. Which was why there were often inappropriate jokes told while standing over the dead. Gallows humor got us through even the toughest of scenes.

Jack and I wound our way to the back of the house toward a spacious and newly renovated kitchen. Mrs. Hargrove was sitting at the kitchen island on a barstool, staring out the big picture window that looked out over a parklike backyard. A mug sat in front of her, still steaming but untouched, but her hands were wrapped around it for warmth.

Walters was leaning against the kitchen counter, sipping out of his own cup. Jack nodded to Walters and we approached Mrs. Hargrove. She didn't seem to notice that we were there.

I looked at Jack and saw the worried expression on his face. Then I took the barstool next to her and gently took her hand, using my fingers to subtly feel the pulse in her wrist.

"Mrs. Hargrove," I said softly. "It's Dr. Graves. Can you look at me?"

She blinked once but that was the only acknowledgment she gave me. Her hands were cold and her pulse fluttered weakly beneath my fingers.

"How long has she been like this?" I asked Walters.

"Not long," he said. "She's been cleaning the kitchen. She made tea and coffee and offered to make me breakfast. And then when she ran out of things to do she just sat down. Maybe five minutes ago. What's wrong?"

"Can you grab a rescue blanket from one of the patrol cars and call in an EMT?" I asked him. "She looks like she's going into shock."

I moved her hot tea out of reach and took her other hand. "Mrs. Hargrove," I said again. "Let's move you to the couch or your bedroom. You need to lie down for me so I can check your vitals. We've got EMTs on the way."

She blinked again, her eyes heavy lidded, as if she were struggling to keep them open. But she finally turned to look at me.

"I'm okay," she said. "I shouldn't have sat down. I always do better when I'm busy. Better not to think about things that way."

Walters came back in with the blanket and we unfolded it, wrapping it around her shoulders. She seemed frail in the moment, and I realized how young she'd been when Jack and I had been her students. Something you don't think about when you're seven years old. She was probably in her late fifties and had always had so much life and vitality in her. Both her and Coach.

"I see a couch right over there," I said, pointing to the closed-in sun porch off the kitchen. It was dark and gloomy as the rain dripped off the glass, but I wanted to put her in a position where I could lay her down quickly and elevate her feet if she got any worse.

Jack helped me get her up and we all moved into the sunroom. It had obviously been a later addition to the house with its bricked floors and white wicker furniture, but I could tell it was well used and probably a place of comfort for her.

"Lydia," I said, once I got her positioned on the couch. "Mrs. Hargrove, can you tell me your address?"

"It's always strange when students call me by my first name," she said, her smile soft and sad. "No matter how long ago they were your students."

"I'm sure it is," I told her, pulling up the ottoman next to her and taking a seat. I kept my fingers on the pulse in her wrist, thankful it was starting to slow and strengthen. She was snuggled into the blanket, drawing in the warmth, and she looked almost childlike beneath it.

"Can you tell me your address?"

"Of course," she said slowly. "1822 Monastery Court. This is my family home. Built in 1901 by my great-grandfather. It'll go to our daughter one day. I haven't called her. I don't think I can."

"Don't worry about that, Mrs. Hargrove," Jack said, taking the wicker chair across from her so she didn't have to turn her head to look at him. "You have people to help you. Lean on us now."

We waited in silence for several minutes as her vitals came back to normal. I still wanted the EMTs to check her out, but she wasn't worrying me as much as she had been when I first saw her.

"We're very proud of you both, you know," she said, breaking the silence. "Steve used to carry around a picture of Jack in his wallet dressed out in his football uniform so he could tell people he used to coach the sheriff. It's been a long time since I've seen either of you. This isn't how I expected our reunion to be."

I saw a flash of color out of the corner of my eye, and watched a couple race across the backyard, carrying a large yellow umbrella. They seemed comfortable coming up the back steps and to the side door of the sunroom, as if they'd done it dozens of times before. The neighbors, I thought.

Jack stood as the door came open and they rushed in. They were a handsome couple. She was as dark as he was pale. Both of them at least six feet tall and athletic looking. I would have put both of them somewhere in their late forties to early fifties.

The woman had a cute pixie cut that was razored at the edges and wore a pair of purple scrubs with yellow daisies on them and white sneakers. The man's hair was an attractive silver, and he wore round glasses, jeans, and an old Yale sweatshirt.

The woman's gaze went between Jack, me, and Lydia, but she ultimately decided now wasn't the time for introductions.

"Oh, Lydia," the woman said, moving toward the couch and leaning over to place her hand on Mrs. Hargrove's cheek affectionately. "We just heard the news. I'm so terribly sorry." Then the woman looked at me out of tawny eyes and said, "Her skin is cold. Does she need to go to the hospital?"

"I've got EMTs on the way to check her out, but her vitals are looking much better and she's able to focus," I said. "You have medical training?"

She smiled, but it was filled with grief. "I'm a nurse at the elementary school. That's how I met Lydia years ago, before she retired. We've been neighbors for a decade and good friends for about the same amount of time."

"Joe Able," Joe said, reaching out to shake Jack's hand. "You're Sheriff Lawson. I've seen you around. That's my wife, Ada. I called Ada at work as soon as your officers left so she could get back home. I knew she'd want to be with Lydia."

Jack nodded. "I'm sure she appreciates that. We need to talk to her and ask some questions. It'll be good you're here."

"You have to ask them now?" Ada asked, her eyes going dark with irritation.

"It's okay," Lydia said, patting Ada's hand. "Sit here next to me. I taught both Jaye and Jack. Smart as whips, both of them. I always knew the two of you would end up together."

I arched a brow at that bit of information and couldn't help a slight smile. "Then you definitely knew more than I did."

Ada took a seat next to Lydia and held one of her hands in both of hers. Joe stayed out of the way, but Jack pushed the chair he'd been in earlier next to me and took a seat.

"You know it's our job to piece together what happened," Jack said. "I know how hard this is and the upcoming days are going to be. But it'll give you peace to know the why of things. As much as we can give you."

Lydia nodded solemnly and she looked down at her entwined hands. "I don't understand it. I don't understand any of this. I can't even believe it's real."

"Was there anything off with his behavior this morning?"

"He was fine," she said. "I know what you're

thinking. That he did this to himself. I saw the gun. I s...saw."

"We don't know anything yet," Jack assured her. "That's why I'm here asking questions. We're going to get to the bottom of this. Coach was the best man I know."

She seemed to collect herself a bit and said, "You knew him. He was big and bold and knew how to get things done. He was a force to be reckoned with. You can't win unless you can see where you're going. And he always knew where he was going. This isn't him. He'd want to win in the end just like he always did. And this isn't winning. It doesn't make sense."

"No, it doesn't," Jack agreed with her, and I saw her shoulders relax a little. "The questions I'm going to ask might seem personal. But we're just eliminating possibilities, and the sooner we can eliminate them the sooner we can get to the truth."

She nodded, and I knew Jack was doing everything he could to put her at ease. No matter how hard we tried to distance ourselves and compartmentalize so the truth could show itself, this was still a woman who helped mold our formative years. She'd always have a special place in our lives.

"Can you walk me through this morning?" Jack asked. "Was it routine?"

"As the sunrise," she said immediately. "Steve was disciplined. This is the off-season so his routine changes in the spring. But he always gets up at four, rain or shine, and he goes to the gym first thing. He uses the one over on Westminster because he says he doesn't want to be in there with a bunch of meatheads who only do arms every day."

Jack chuckled. "I don't blame him. That's a good gym. They're open twenty-four seven if I recall."

"He likes that too," she said. "He wants to get in and out early in the mornings. He'll usually drive through and get coffee for both of us on his way home." Her lips pressed together. "He did this morning. He brought me a caramel latte. It's my favorite. I don't get up as early as I used to. I retired a couple of years ago. But I was up by the time he got back. It was a little before six. We sat out here and drank our coffee and watched the sun come up."

Her voice hitched and Ada put her arm around Lydia's shoulders, pulling her into an embrace.

"I didn't realize it would be the last time," she said. "I would have stayed longer. But I wanted to get showered and get to the store and back before the rain came in. I always do my grocery shopping on Fridays. Martin's Grocery gets their produce in fresh Thursday night, so I shop on Friday mornings."

"What time did you get back home?" Jack asked.

"I'm not sure," she said. "Maybe around seven thirty? I was surprised to see Steve's car still parked in the driveway. He usually leaves for school around six forty-five."

"It's okay, Mrs. Hargrove," he said. "Take your time."

"I figured if Steve was still home he could help me bring in the groceries," she said. "But then when I came inside I could smell...I could smell, and I thought maybe he was sick and that's why he hadn't left for school yet. I saw his things sitting by the front door, like he was ready to walk out, so I checked the powder bath off the living room first. But it was empty. So I went to his study."

She looked up at us then, her eyes wide and wet, her face ashen. "I just don't understand. He wouldn't do that."

"Was the exterior door locked when you came home?" Jack asked.

She shook her head. "We never lock the

doors in this neighborhood. Most of us have been here a long time and we tend to pop in and out of each other's houses. I always have a pot of coffee on for company."

"Did Steve get any phone calls or news that upset him? Anything out of the ordinary?"

"Not this morning," she said, biting her lip in thought.

"Another day recently?" he pressed.

"He's been having meetings this week with administration and his staff. He's been having problems with one of his coaches and Steve ultimately decided it was time for him to be let go because it was what's best for the team. You know how things work here. It doesn't take long for word to travel through the grapevine, and Archie heard from one of the school board members about his termination before Steve could talk to him face-to-face. Archie called and lit into Steve, and then later that night Archie showed up at the house and was banging on the door for a while. We were at our daughter's house for dinner, so we saw it on the doorbell camera." She looked down at her hands again. "I'm glad we weren't home."

"What night was this?" Jack asked.

"Wednesday night," she answered.

"Do you know Archie's last name?"

"Hill," she said.

I saw the EMTs heading our way and waved them in. Mrs. Hargrove was looking pale and frail again, and I knew our time with her was up.

"What do I do?" she asked, grabbing my hand as I stood to make way for the medical personnel. "I don't know what to do without Steve."

"Let the people who love you take care of you," I told her. "Let's get you checked out and then Ada can pack some things for you and get you settled somewhere else for a few days."

"You can come stay with me," Ada said. "We've got the guest room all ready for you. And we'll go see Livvy. You don't want her hearing things from other people."

"You're right," Lydia said. "I need to go to my daughter and we'll all deal with this together."

We said our goodbyes, and made our way back through the house. The techs were still working, and Lily and Sheldon were working alongside them, meticulously scraping and bagging pieces of Steve Hargrove.

I let the grief wash over me, knowing the chances were likely this was a suicide. But hoping, for everyone's sake, that it was a murder.

CHAPTER THREE

ONCE WE HAD COACH HARGROVE LOADED INTO the Suburban, Jack followed me back to the funeral home and helped me unload. This was not in his job description, but we all tended to pitch in where needed on short staff and short funds.

"Too early for lunch," Jack said, washing his hands in the kitchen sink.

"I was just thinking that," I said. "It feels like we put a full day in already. We can always do brunch."

"I like the way you think," he said, leaning down to give me a quick kiss.

Before either of us could come up with a suggestion on where we should eat, Jack's phone rang. I could tell by the look on his face it was dispatch.

"Lawson," he said, listening for several seconds before saying, "No, she's here with me. I'll put you on speaker."

He put his phone down on the bar and hit the speaker button. "Go ahead, dispatch."

"I've had three calls come in the last five minutes," Barbara said. "All of them doozies. I've got a guy who was doused in gasoline and set on fire, an old guy who kicked the bucket during sex, and a body that washed up in Gambo Creek."

"You got three dead bodies in the last five minutes?" Jack asked.

"It's a full moon tonight," Barbara said. "And Friday the thirteenth. What do you expect? I've got crosses and Virgin Marys all over my console. I don't want any of that demon stuff coming here."

Jack sighed.

"Besides," she went on. "There's only two official bodies. The guy that got set on fire isn't dead. Yet."

"Give Martinez death by sex," Jack said. "He just left the Hargrove scene. Call in Cole for burning man. And Jaye and I will take the body in Gambo Creek. Send me the location on my phone."

"10-4," Barbara said.

I could tell she was ramping up to say more, but Jack disconnected before any words came out.

"Gonna be a busy day," he said, rubbing his hand over his head. "No time for a haircut."

"It's gonna be a busy several days," I said. "I've got at least three autopsies waiting for me. Four if burning man doesn't make it. I picked a bad day to throw away my donuts."

Jack was feeling merciful, so he drove through a chain coffee shop on our way to Gambo Creek. I was pretty sure he needed the caffeine kick too, so it wasn't completely sacrificial.

The rain had steadily increased, so on top of the service calls we were making, Jack was also having to coordinate officers so they could shut down the roads that were flooding. This area had a lot of creeks and rivers, some of them flowing into the Potomac, but many of them didn't have a natural drainage system so bridges frequently washed out when the rain got too bad.

Jack didn't have an easy job, but he made it

look effortless. As sheriff, he was always working and always on call. And while I knew this in my head, Jack did a great job of making me feel like it was just us when we were home. His responsibility was great.

Gambo Creek ran through Bloody Mary and King George Proper, and it widened the closer it got to the Potomac River before they merged. The address Barbara had sent us was in King George, but there was no telling where the body had been dumped, especially with the water rising.

We took Jack's 4x4 truck to the crime scene, and we were going at a snail's pace over the Raddock Bridge. The water had risen and it wouldn't be long until the bridge was closed completely.

"We're going to have to make this quick," I said. "The last thing we want is to be trapped on the wrong side of the river."

"We've got time yet," Jack said. "Though you'll probably need the EMTs to transport. I doubt Lily will have time to get out here with the Suburban."

"She's going to be occupied for a bit," I said. "She and Cole seem to be in a good place. I think she's all but moved in with him. I don't remember the last time she didn't leave work to head to his place."

"You seem surprised," Jack said.

"I am. This is the longest relationship Cole's ever had. It's a good thing."

"The right woman has a tendency to have that effect on a man," Jack said. "Do you want to talk about it?"

"Talk about what?" I asked, knowing exactly what he was referring to.

He kept his eyes on the road, but I felt the air go out of him. "I saw the pregnancy test in the trash can."

I shrugged, hiding my face behind my to-go cup and scalding my tongue for my troubles. "It's not the first I've taken," I said. "I'm sure it won't be the last."

"You didn't tell me," he said.

"There's no reason to get both of our hopes up." I shifted uncomfortably in my seat, tugging at the seat belt that was choking the life out of me all of a sudden. There was awkward silence between us and then I finally said, "I just thought I would try. And if it was positive I would surprise you. And if negative…no harm, no foul."

"I know," he said. "We've not been trying that long. We've just got to give it some time. There's no pressure to do this by a certain time or date.

It'll happen when it happens. Like Reverend Thomas says, 'God's timing and our timing aren't always the same.'"

I snorted out a laugh. "When Reverend Thomas has his sherry at night he also says he can see angels dancing in his bedroom."

Jack chuckled and he waved at the deputy assigned at the edge of the road, sitting in his unit with the lights flashing and windshield wipers swishing. Jack and I had both put on our rain gear before we'd left the funeral home, but we were still going to get wet. Being wet was one of my least favorite things, just behind being strangled and being shot at.

A police barricade had been set up and an ambulance was parked off to the side per standard procedure.

"Here we go," I said, pulling up my hood and tying it tightly to keep the rain off my head.

The wind blew the car door open and my rain boots squished down in the mud, making sucking sounds as we made our way to the edge of the creek. It was a heavily treed area and there was a lot of underbrush on both sides of the creek. There weren't any major roads out here, and the closest neighborhood was at least a mile away.

I nodded at Chen, noticing she looked wet

and annoyed, and I wondered if her having real sugar had made any difference in her overall attitude. It didn't seem like it.

"This is the middle of nowhere," I said. "How'd the body get discovered?"

"A guy named Robert Madison called it in," Chen said. "He said his dogs were outside and freaked out when they heard the thunder. They dug under the fence and took off before he could bring them back inside. Dogs found the body."

"Animals always add a nice addition to autopsy findings," I said. "All the extra bite marks and saliva are super helpful."

"The victim washed up and got caught in the underbrush there," Chen said, pointing to a spiny shrub with sticks and other debris caught in it. "As you can see, it's mostly under water, so we had to move her to higher ground. She was starting to shift and I was afraid she was going to keep going down creek."

"That's a good call," I said. "And it doesn't matter too much at this point. There's no telling how long she's been in the water and how far she's travelled. Looks like you drew the short straw for this one."

"I disagree," she said. "I already heard about Plank having to change uniforms. I'm okay with a little rain. I guess it's a good thing I already ate my donuts for fortification."

"That's just mean, Chen," I said, narrowing my eyes at her. "I didn't know you had it in you."

"I'm from Atlanta," she said as if that explained everything.

I wiped water from my eyes and trudged my way to the blue tarp near the base of a tree, my boots making a squelching sound with every step. I pulled back the tarp and got my first look at the victim.

"She's young," I said. "Maybe early twenties. Caucasian female, multiple lacerations, probably postmortem due to her trip down the creek, but we'll get them all sorted out in the lab."

Water was never kind to anyone when they'd been submerged for a lengthy amount of time. Her skin was blue and mottled and her eyes were open and stared blankly. Gnarled blond hair was tangled with twigs and leaves. There was no jewelry around her neck or on her fingers. Her nails and toes were painted pale pink.

"She's wearing a nightgown," Jack said.

"With all due respect," Chen said. "That is not a nightgown. My wai po wears a nightgown. It's flannel and ugly. This is a sex gown."

"I was trying to be respectful," Jack said.

"It's amazing there's any of it left," I said.

"This is one of those expensive nighties. Flimsy lace and silk. Matching panties. Which are intact it seems. Looks like the gown snagged everything on the way down the creek. Nothing holding it to her body except water.

"If she did have sex there won't be any seminal evidence left," I said. "I can look for tears or signs of force, but that's about it. She's got multiple stab wounds in her chest and abdomen."

"That's a date that went wrong," Chen said.

"Understatement," I said. "There's no needle marks. Or none obvious. She looks like she took good care of herself. Good musculature. Probably worked out. Upper middle class at least."

"Someone will be missing her," Jack said. "Shouldn't be too hard to find out who she is. There's no identification."

"Not unless it's shoved somewhere I don't want to look right now," I said. "We'll be lucky if we find any evidence on the body. You might have better luck searching the banks to see if anything else got dumped with her."

"This rain is getting on my nerves," Jack said. "Half this county is about to be blocked in. The Weather Channel said we're having a hundred-year flood."

"Yeah," Chen said. "I passed that meteorologist guy who always goes to the worst weather locations by the park this morning. That's never a good sign."

I signaled to the EMT that I was ready for him and was glad to see a familiar face. "How's it going, Percy?" I asked.

"Could be better," he said. "Caught this at the end of my twelve hours."

I winced in sympathy. "Isn't that the way it always happens. Guess you haven't learned to pretend you're in the bathroom during that last call at end of shift."

"Believe me," he said, putting the stretcher down next to the victim. "I've used it. But you can't overuse it. I'm already on my third time this month. Usually I let the rookie take these. He needs the practice. But it's his kid's birthday today, so I told him to head home."

"That's why they call you a hero," I said deadpan.

Percy snorted and called out to his partner who was opening the back of the ambulance. "Hey, Henry, let's get out of here before we're all washed down the river."

Percy pulled an electronic device out of his pocket, clicked a couple of boxes, and then handed it for me to sign.

"Thank God for technology," he said. "Paper

release forms on a clipboard wouldn't have done it today."

I signed for the transport and release of the body, and then he shoved the device back inside his jumpsuit.

Percy and Henry lifted the woman onto the stretcher and then carried her to the back of the ambulance, sliding her in and slamming the doors shut.

"Catch you on the other side," Percy said.

"Ahh, Friday the thirteenth ," Chen said. We watched the red lights of the ambulance as they pulled away.

"Yeah," I said. "And just think, the full moon isn't even out yet."

CHAPTER FOUR

"DO YOU BELIEVE IN ALL THAT STUFF?" I ASKED Jack on the way back to the funeral home. "The superstitions of Friday the thirteenth and the full moon. Do you think that's why we're being slammed with bodies?"

"Nope," he said. "But people are people, and it's easier to put a label on things. Everyone has a label for everything nowadays. I heard on the news this morning that a Friday the thirteenth full moon only occurs once every twenty years. That's plenty of time for people to amp themselves up, to watch their violent horror movies, jump at shadows and let their imaginations go crazy. Dates and triggers and memories...they do something to people and sometimes they just snap. You can't always explain everything. Maybe that's why Christmas and New Year are the highest murder days of the year."

He pulled into the driveway at the funeral home behind the ambulance. "I need to get back and check on the flooding issues. You got it from here?"

"Yeah," I said, leaning over to give him a quick kiss. "I guess I'll see you when I see you."

"Eat something healthy to offset all the coffee you've had," he said. "You can't live on caffeine alone."

"Filthy lies," I said, looking horrified. "I'm a doctor. I know these things." I winked at him and pushed my way out of the truck and back into the rain and wind.

I let Percy and Henry do the heavy lifting, so to speak, and get our Jane Doe into the lab that occupied the basement of Graves Funeral Home. My parents had operated the funeral home before me, so I'd never questioned where they worked. What I hadn't realized was that they had a Frankenstein kind of lab set up where they were smuggling everything from money to weapons inside the bodies.

The security was tighter than Fort Knox and the equipment was top of the line. You could afford the best of everything when your criminal enterprise was successful.

Once they'd gotten her downstairs, I signed the device again for receipt of Jane Doe, and then followed them back upstairs. "Feel free to grab something to drink. There's sodas in the refrigerator. Or water."

"We are leaving and turning our phones and radios off," Percy said, giving me a two-fingered salute. "This shift is officially over."

"I hear you," I said, and Percy and Henry were on their way.

I stripped out of my rain gear and boots and stashed them in the mudroom to dry out. I locked the door since I was going to be down in the lab, knowing Lily and Sheldon could get in using the code. And then, out of guilt, I rummaged around in the refrigerator, thinking Jack and Emmy Lu must be in cahoots, because it was stocked with things I wouldn't eat on a normal basis.

I pulled out a bowl of hummus and sliced veggies, and then didn't feel guilty for starting another pot of coffee. I carried my plate to my office just off the kitchen and snacked on a carrot while I stripped out of my wet clothes and put on a pair of black leggings and a thin black sweater. And then I shoved my feet into sneakers because I was going to be standing for a while.

The funeral home was quiet, which wasn't

unusual, but I hadn't seen the Suburban in the parking lot so I assumed Lily and Sheldon were still at the Hargrove house. Emmy Lu's minivan was parked in her spot, and she was probably tucked away in her office. She'd have seen me come in on the cameras. Emmy Lu didn't miss much.

I did feel more energized after eating, so I grabbed another cup of coffee and then headed downstairs. It was cold in the lab, and I grabbed my lab coat off the hook out of habit, pulling it on over my clothes, and then I grabbed a heavy canvas apron to put on top of that. There was no such thing as too much protection. I'd seen some weird things happen with bodies over the years.

I decided to wait on Coach Hargrove. He was fine in the refrigeration unit until Lily and Sheldon got back, and then we could start piecing him together again. But for now, my focus was on the Jane Doe.

There was something about the unidentified victims that made me want to work harder to see justice done. No one deserved to go nameless, as if their life had never existed. They had families and memories that deserved to be honored, and the faster I could put a name to her face, the better.

Percy and Henry had transferred her onto the

large metal table I used for autopsies. She lay pale, the blue of her veins making her skin look like marble. The lividity in her body wasn't unusual for someone who'd been tossed in a creek. The head, arms and legs tended to hang forward, so she would have been face down in the water, which was why all her blood had pooled in the front of her body.

The white nightie was twisted around her waist, what was left of it tinged pink with blood. I removed it carefully, documenting the brand and size, and then doing the same with her underwear.

I turned on my playlist to fill the empty space. Nat King Cole came out from the speakers and I hummed along to "Nature Boy" as I collected every piece of debris that still clung to her body and put it in a sterile tray.

I took her body temperature, which didn't mean much since she'd been submerged in water, but her body wasn't badly decomposed like someone who'd been in the water for weeks, and she was only slightly bloated. I had some other suspicions about her death as well, but I wouldn't know for certain until I cut her open. And I'd be able to narrow the window of time of death from her organ decomposition.

"Thirteen stab wounds," I said, meticulously

noting them on the body chart. I measured each one in length and depth. "One weapon. Serrated edge. Whoever killed you was very angry. Each one got a little deeper. It got a little easier every time they stabbed you."

She had abrasions on her hands and feet, her cheeks, knees, hips—all consistent with her trip down the river. But there was a contusion along her left jaw—a discoloring of green and purple—consistent with a blow to the face that was most definitely perimortem.

Once I finished with her exterior, I took x-rays, and then I turned off the music and turned on my recorder so I could make notes without taking the chance of dropping my pen in an open cavity.

It wasn't long after I'd cut her open that my suspicions were confirmed. Official cause of death was not the thirteen stab wounds in her chest and stomach that had somehow managed to miss major arteries that would've caused her to bleed out quickly.

I collected a sample of water and mud and algae from her lungs and labeled them. Cause of death was drowning. She was still alive when her killer had thrown her in the river. After the body dies and oxygen stops flowing to the brain, we go through what's called autolysis. We literally start to self-digest and our cells start eating themselves from the inside out. Even with her being submerged in water and not having an accurate body temp, I knew she'd probably been dead somewhere around thirty to sixty hours.

There wasn't a lot to put in Jane Doe's file. I knew she was unmarried and had never given birth. I knew she was at least twenty-three years old because her sacrum was fused together. I knew she'd broken her leg as a child and it had been expertly set and healed properly. I knew she was either a student or worked at a desk job from the curvature of her neck and spine—she was someone who spent long hours at a desk or computer—but she also spent time in the gym based on her musculature. And I knew she'd been violently stabbed and tossed into the river like a piece of trash, where she'd eventually died.

I was hoping Jack would be able to tell me more.

I'd lost track of time, so I was surprised when I heard someone keying in the code and opening the heavy reinforced door upstairs.

"I suppose I should thank you for the hands-on experience," Lily called out. "But I'm not there yet."

"Understandable," I said.

"I will say it's easy to stay skinny in this job," Lily said. "I don't think I'm going to be able to eat for another couple of weeks."

"As long as you can still drink water, you should be able to live without food for approximately fifty to seventy days," Sheldon said. "Angus Barbieri holds the record for going three hundred and eighty-two days without food. He lived on tea, soda, and vitamins. But he was Scottish, so maybe that had something to do with it."

"Thanks, Sheldon," Lily said. "That's good information in case I want to choose a slow and painful way to die or beat a world record."

I hid my smile and turned the music down as they tromped down the metal stairs like a couple of kids coming home from school. Sheldon was my assistant at the funeral home. He was brilliant on the mortuary side of the business. His people skills...lacked.

He trailed after Lily like a lost puppy. I could tell by the look on his face he wasn't sure if she was being sarcastic about choosing to die a slow and painful death. Sheldon was an acquired taste. He was a thirty-year-old man who lived at home with his mother and looked like the Pillsbury Doughboy. He wore Coke-bottle-thick glasses, had a comb-over, and he was the champion of useless trivia.

"Crime scene guys are finished too," Lily said. "Some of the buckshot is in our remains, so we'll need to get that back over to ballistics as soon as we can. But we got everything." Lily patted the box she carried before setting it on the table. "You wouldn't believe some of the places we found brain matter. It's crazy what buckshot can do to soft tissue."

"I didn't throw up," Sheldon said.

"Always a step in the right direction," I told him. "The crime scene techs hate that."

"I'm going back upstairs," he said abruptly. "The viewing rooms will be open soon."

"Hey, I heard back from the gravediggers," I told him as he went back upstairs. "They were able to get the graves dug before the weather came in, but their excavator got stuck in the mud in the cemetery, so I'm sure you'll hear complaints from Mrs. Lichner that we should have covered the excavator with flowers so it didn't ruin her graveside backdrop."

"I don't like that woman," Sheldon said. "She keeps patting the top of my head every time she asks for something. I have sensitive follicles. I had a dream last night I pushed her into the grave on top of her husband."

"Did he push her back out?" Lily asked. "He probably wants some peace in the afterlife."

I laughed and pulled Steve Hargrove out of the refrigeration unit to go through the preliminaries of the autopsy.

"Why don't you start with the skull," I told Lily. "Don't remove any particles or buckshot yet. Just see what pieces of the skull we have and get them laid out. And you pick the music."

"I'm on a Billie Eilish kick," Lily said. "But sometimes her songs can be real downers, so we might have to change to Taylor Swift."

Lily was a rare unicorn. She was one of the most beautiful women I'd ever seen, and I knew she'd modeled some in high school and college. She was close to six feet tall and had a long fall of black hair that reached the middle of her back. Her eyes were vivid blue and her body looked like it came from a Kardashian's plastic surgeon. She had looks, but you'd never know by talking to her that she thought she had looks. Her kindness and humility were right up there with her brains. She had it all.

I remembered my first year of medical school, and I didn't recall having it together like Lily did. She was working, going to school full-time, and she was dating a man seventeen years older than she was. Twenty-three-year-old me had been an underachiever compared to Lily.

"Right," I said, not having a clue about either artist, but typing their names into my phone to make a new playlist. I put it on low volume in the background so I could still give a verbal assessment as I did the autopsy.

I pulled on a fresh pair of gloves and used the magnifier to go over every inch of Coach Hargrove's clothes. I removed his shoes and bagged them, noting the spatter and taking a swab to make sure the blood was his. I removed his wedding ring and watch, bagging them so they could be returned to his wife. And then I removed the remainder of his clothing and hung them up inside a compartment with a tray at the bottom. I pressed the button and a low hum sounded as the clothes gently vibrated. I'd check it later to see if any particles or evidence had fallen into the tray.

From the neck down, Coach Hargrove looked like a perfectly healthy fifty-nine-year-old man. I took x-rays, and then I pulled the magnifier down and went over every inch of his skin, looking for something that indicated he was lying on my table because someone else put him there. I swabbed his hands for gunshot residue and it came back positive. Coach Hargrove was definitely holding the weapon that killed him. Not a good sign.

He was in great shape, there was nothing abnormal in his blood work, and his organs showed a man who took care of himself and ate right. He was someone who should've had a long life ahead of him.

"Coffee, raisins, wheat, brown sugar and milk in his stomach," I said.

Lily squenched her nose. "Raisin Bran? Not what I'd choose for my last meal."

"Me either," I said, taking out organs and weighing them, and then putting them back.

"I keep finding these weird flecks," Lily said a few minutes later. "Particles mixed in with the tissue. We must have scraped too hard and mixed fibers."

I came over to the sterile metal table where she had Steve Hargrove's brain, skull, and other fleshy pieces like his nose lined up and labeled.

"What do you mean flecks?" I asked, pulling down the overhead light so I could get a better view.

"It's embedded in the occipital. It looks like red glitter," she said. "I don't know. It's weird. Maybe there was glitter in the carpet?"

"Maybe," I said, looking through the microscope. There were several shiny red flakes just like she'd said. "Grab an evidence bag and we'll send these off to be analyzed. Have you found them anywhere else?"

"On that piece," she said. "But I'm not sure what part of the skull it is yet. It's fleshy. And brainy."

"Parietal," I said, turning the fragments carefully in my hand. "You can barely see the suture line."

There was too much damage to the flesh around the pieces of skull I was holding. It was like holding a mangled piece of beef. I took the tweezers and painstakingly removed all the flecks I could find and dropped them in the bag Lily held open.

We spent the next couple of hours extracting buckshot from tissue and bone and then putting as much of Coach Hargrove together as we could.

"There's still a good part of the skull that's missing," I said. "It was a twelve-pellet load of buckshot in the shotgun. We recovered eight pellets from his soft tissue. I'll check with Jack to see if the techs picked up the remaining four. But the initial shotgun blast through the soft tissue of the underside of the chin means that those twelve pellets made soup out of Hargrove's head. We've got pieces of flesh with shotgun residue, and swab tests on his right hand came back positive as well. So we know he was holding the weapon at the time it was fired."

"Not looking good for anything but suicide," Lily said.

"Yeah, but those red flakes are weird. And the flesh is too damaged. Let's clean up the remaining pieces of skull and bone, strip the flesh, and then see what's under there," I told her. "While you do that, I'm going to run these things over to the crime lab."

Lily grunted. "I don't have anywhere else to be," she said.

I stripped off my gloves and took off my apron and lab coat. "Yeah, I heard Cole got pulled in on the guy who got doused in gasoline and set on fire. That seems fitting for a full moon. But maybe he won't be too late. The last I heard the guy survived."

"That seems worse somehow," she said.

"I can't disagree," I told her. "Text me if anything new comes up."

CHAPTER FIVE

I'D LOST TRACK OF TIME DOWN IN THE BASEMENT, and I noticed it was past five by the time I got back upstairs and gathered all my things. The parking lot at the funeral home was full as the viewings for Merilee Walling and Bruce Lichner were well underway. The side of the funeral home with my office and the lab was blocked off from the viewing public, so I was able to slip out without notice.

It was still a couple of hours shy of sunset, but the sky was the same dark and gloomy gray it had been all day. The rain had let up a little so I could see other cars on the road as I made my way over to the sheriff's office. I was assuming Jack would be there, but he could just as likely have been out on a call or dealing with the flooding.

Thoughts of flooding made me wonder if we'd be able to get to our own house, or if we'd be sleeping in the little room behind Jack's office. Heresy Road was elevated, situated parallel on the cliffs overlooking the Potomac River. It was getting up to Heresy Road that was the problem.

But I'd never known anything different. I'd grown up on Heresy Road, in an old Victorian that had been filled with miserable memories and rotting wood. When Jack and I had married, I'd moved two miles down the road to his place. The memories were much better and there was no rotting wood in sight. It had been a long time since the river had risen so high that we couldn't cross the bridge to get home. It had maybe happened twice in my lifetime. I was hoping this wasn't going to be a third.

All the parking spots were filled in front of the sheriff's office, including Jack's, and I had to park across the street at the courthouse. I grabbed my bag, double-checked to make sure the evidence was safely tucked inside, and I hurried across the street.

My speed didn't matter much. It seemed I was going to live in a constant state of damp this spring. I squeezed between police cars and up the front steps to the big glass double doors emblazoned with *King George County Sheriff's Office* in neat white letters.

The lobby area and waiting room were filled with people, all talking at various degrees of volume. It was pure chaos. There were deputies stationed by the interior doors that led to the bullpen and holding areas, and then there was Sergeant Hill sitting behind the Plexiglass partition, not ruffled by anything and as stoic as ever. His bushy mustache hardly twitched as he processed people in and took names for those waiting to make reports.

"Busy night," I said, waving to Hill as I waited for the deputy to let me into the inner sanctum.

"Full moon," he said. "We haven't seen anything yet."

"Comforting," I said, thanking the deputy.

I walked down the short corridor that led to the bullpen and Jack's office. It wasn't any quieter in this part of the station, but the sounds were different. The phones were constantly ringing, cops were taking statements, and others were grabbing their coats and heading for the exit.

"Hey, Doc," Durrant called out. "Crazy day, huh?"

"Hill says we haven't seen anything yet," I said.

"He should know," Durrant said. "Hill's dad is a priest and his mom is a voodoo priestess. He's got the sight."

"That would explain a lot about Hill," I said.

"I think he gets the mustache from his mom," Durrant said.

I grinned and detoured my way to the opposite end of the room where forensics was located. There was a gray door with a frosted-glass window, and across the window was the word *FORENSICS* in black block letters, only the *O* was slightly out of alignment and it always made me a little cross eyed to look at it.

I was hoping my favorite lab tech was on duty, but the forensics guys were kind of like mole people—they lived in the dark, came out at weird times of day, and people generally forgot they were there unless they needed them for something.

I stepped inside the cave and let my eyes adjust to the darkness. It smelled like burnt coffee, corn chips, and pineapple.

"Is Cheney in?" I asked.

There was a pale man hunched over a desk, looking at fingerprint samples. He was short and stocky and had a mop of black curly hair on top of his head. He was dressed in jeans and a sweatshirt. I didn't know all of the crime scene techs, but I recognized most of them on sight. The forensics teams weren't cops, so only a few of them were licensed to carry weapons. Which was probably a good thing.

"She's back at her desk," he said. "But she's in a mood."

"Everyone is today," I said. "Why does it smell like pineapple?"

"Wojcinski likes pineapple on her pizza," he said. "But Cheney made her go to the big break-room instead of ours cause she said only communists eat pineapple on pizza and communists aren't allowed in the forensics lab."

"Good to know the rules," I said, heading down to Cheney's office.

Cindy Cheney reminded me of SpongeBob SquarePants. She was perfectly rectangular. Her mousy brown hair looked like it had been given a home haircut and her lips were pinched tight as she looked through a microscope.

I knocked on the frame of her door and she grunted. "I've got some things for you," I said.

"If some of those things don't include dinner for two at Patrizio's and an ultimate spa day filled with sexual favors, then make an appointment for some time next week."

"I can do Patrizio's and a massage," I told her.

"You'll have to ask Martinez about the sexual favors. That's not my wheelhouse."

"Wouldn't matter anyway," she said, pushing away from her desk. "I usually fall asleep during a massage anyway. I'm too old for all that other crap. Heard you caught the Hargrove case. That's a shame he went out like that. My daughter had him in high school. He was a good man."

This was high praise coming from Cheney. She wasn't one to be overly complimentary.

"That's what I want you to look at," I said, handing over the labeled bag with the red flecks. "Found these embedded in parts of his skull. Lily thought they might have been scraped up by accident when they collected the rest of him from the scene."

"I'll take a look," she said. "What's all this other crap?"

"Samples from my Jane Doe and the remaining buckshot for ballistics."

"Did you submit them for processing?" she asked, "Or am I going to have to do that too?"

"Patrizio's and a spa day," I told her, backing out of her office. "You're the best, Cheney."

I hurried out of forensics, knowing Cheney would start on the samples I'd given her. She was a widow and lived and breathed the job. I assumed it was easier than going home to an empty house. Can't say I blamed her all that much.

Once I was back out in the bullpen I let my eyes adjust and then headed toward Jack's office. King George County wasn't by any stretch the most populous county in Virginia. We had just under thirty thousand residents, according to the last census, which had worked out well because the sheriff's department had been way under-staffed in the ten years since the previous census. Jack now had a department of more than a hundred and twenty sworn officers, plus admin-istrators, lab techs, K-9s, and corrections officers. And me.

It was an intense operation to keep running, and I couldn't imagine what it was like at the big city level. And it looked like every cop and auxil-iary person on payroll was on duty.

Jack's office door was open, and as soon as I stepped inside he hung up the phone and stood up from behind his desk.

"I think I've got an identity for our Jane Doe," he said. "Cami Downey. Reported missing by her roommate this morning. She's a law clerk for Judge Stevens. Age twenty-four."

"Time of death is somewhere between thirty and sixty hours," I said. "She wasn't in the water long. Official cause of death is drowning."

Jack raised his brows at that. "She was alive when she went in the water?"

"Thirteen stab wounds and not one of them nicked any major arteries," I said. "She had organ damage, but it would have been treatable had she gotten to a hospital in time."

"Downey's address is in King George Proper, not too far from campus."

"Plenty of dump spots around there into Gambo Creek," I said. "Her killer was probably hoping she'd be washed into the Potomac. That would've put a wrench in things."

"We're lucky she didn't," Jack said. "With the rising water there were all kinds of obstacles to slow her down."

"What's the plan?" I asked.

"I want to swing by and talk to Archie Hill," Jack said. "He should be home by now. And then we can grab something to eat and check out Cami Downey's roommate."

"Hey, boss," Martinez said, knocking on the door and letting himself inside. "You got a minute for me to brief you on the old guy?"

"What do you have?"

"Victim is seventy-eight-year-old Rooney Danforth," Martinez said. "And his new wife is the same age as his granddaughter. They got married about six months ago. According to

Peyton—that's the new wife—old Rooney was getting the ride of his life when he grabbed his chest and said he was having a heart attack.

"Peyton says she didn't take him seriously at first because he's an enthusiastic lover and sometimes he likes to roleplay." Martinez stopped and stuck his finger in his mouth to make a gagging motion. "So Peyton kept the rodeo going until his face turned red and he was no longer responsive. That's when she jumped up and called 911."

"Find anything unusual?" Jack asked.

"Not on the surface," Martinez said. "Airtight prenup was signed before the wedding. Wife walks away with two hundred and fifty Gs and the marital home. The rest goes to his kids and a bunch of charities. The kids hate her, but that's to be expected. The wife did say they'd been trying to have a baby. Said he does take performance enhancement drugs and he'd just had a whiskey before they started doing the deed. Body is being sent to you, Doc."

"Lily is at the lab," I told him. "She can sign for him."

"Seems pretty cut and dry," Martinez said, shrugging. "But we'll see what you squeeze out of him, Doc."

I winced and said, "Poor choice of words, Martinez."

He just laughed and backed out the door. "I'm taking Plank out for dinner. I told him if he buys I won't make fun of him for brains falling on his face this morning. Poor kid still has tissue up his nose."

"Make sure you bag it if any comes out," I said.

"I'm not bagging Plank's snot," Martinez said. "He could buy me all the dinners in the world and I still wouldn't do that."

I grunted and waved bye to Martinez. Jack pulled on his police issue Gore-Tex jacket and the matching pants. He kicked off his regular boots and laced up his SWAT boots since they were waterproof.

"I feel underdressed," I said.

"I've been all over this county today. I'm tired of being wet. I'm growing mold in places I don't want to think about it."

"Lovely visual image," I said. "Now I'm thinking about it too."

"Misery loves company. Let's roll out."

Archie Hill lived in one of the older neighborhoods in Nottingham. It was a shotgun house on a street of identical vinyl-siding shotgun homes. They all had box hedges in front and miniscule front lawns. Teachers got paid about as much as cops did in the state of

Virginia, so it looked like a house that a teacher could afford.

"This guy isn't originally from here," I said. "What's the story?"

Jack smiled and said, "I guess it depends on how much of the story is true. From what I've pieced together, Hill and his wife and kid moved here four years ago from Richmond. He was a head coach at one of the big high schools."

"Sounds like he downgraded," I said.

"This is direct gossip from Barbara so take it or leave it," he said.

"Oh, I definitely want to hear it," I said. "We can sort out the details later." Gossip was like mother's milk in a small town, but it was something we were never weaned off of.

"According to Barbara." Then he paused and said, "And we know she's almost never wrong. Hill was having an affair with one of the other teachers. I guess his wife found out about it..."

"As they always do," I said, cutting in.

"And they decided a change of location was necessary," Jack continued. "Coach Hargrove makes the hire, thinking he's getting a stacked deck in his coaching staff, but Hill has head coach mentality. He and the wife stick it out for a couple of years, and then during training camp this past summer she packs up the daughter and goes back to her parents in Richmond. And then last week he finds out his contract isn't being renewed and loses what little self-control he has left."

"Sounds like a man pushed to the breaking point," I said. "If Hargrove was directly involved with him not being rehired then we've got a motive. But still no means and opportunity if Hargrove didn't kill himself. And unless Lily comes up with a smoking gun in the next few hours, I'm going to have to rule it suicide. I can't hold him on ice forever because we want it to be something else."

"I know," Jack said. "We'll see how it plays out. Let's go get a close-up look at Coach Hill."

Jack parked his unit behind an old tan F-150. I tossed my hood over my head and we hurried up to the porch. There was a leak in the awning over the door and a steady *splat splat splat* hit the cement stairs. There were no plants or flower-pots, no toys or any other visible signs that a woman or child lived there.

"Yeah," Hill said as he opened the front door and leaned against the threshold. His arm hung down at his side and he held a bottle of beer between two fingers. "Can I help you?"

"I'm Sheriff Lawson," Jack said, showing him his badge. "And this is Dr. Graves. She's the coroner for King George County. Are you Archie Hill?"

"That's me," he said. "I know who you are. What's this about?"

"We'd like to ask you some questions about Steve Hargrove."

Hill stared at Jack for a few seconds and then pushed open the door a little wider. "I figured. Heard he offed himself this morning. We've not made an official announcement at school, but you hear things. Kids are pretty shook up about it. The principal is holding a special meeting for staff and students tomorrow morning."

"Steve Hargrove's death is still an open investigation," Jack said, taking a look around the small room.

There was one recliner and a big-screen TV on the wall. He was using a television tray as an end table and there were several empty beer bottles sitting around. There was no other furniture in the room.

"Sorry I can't offer you a seat," he said. "My wife took everything in the divorce."

"We won't take up much of your time," Jack said.

Hill grabbed the remote and put the TV on mute. "What does open investigation mean?" he asked.

"It means we haven't ruled cause of death yet," I said. "We don't have conclusive evidence from the body, which means we have to conduct it as a homicide."

"I see," he said. "So you heard my contract didn't get renewed and figured that gives me a reason to kill the guy?"

"We heard your contract didn't get renewed," Jack said calmly. "And that you were pretty angry with Coach Hargrove so you called him. You even showed up at his house a couple of nights ago. We've got it captured on the doorbell camera."

"So what?" he asked. "Yeah, I'm pissed. I pour four years into this program. Lose my marriage and my daughter. All with the understanding that Steve is going to retire at the end of this year and I would take over as head coach. Steve's glory days are in the past. We've got an incredible team. I mean, freaking Derek Able already has scouts at every game and practice he's at. I've not seen a quarterback like him in my entire career. And yet we're not winning state championships."

"Why is that?" Jack asked.

"Cause Hargrove lost his nerve," Hill said. "He's got a lot of years and a lot of experience. But when you don't adapt to your players and the changes in the game, you reach a threshold and that's as good as you'll ever do. He's stuck in the past. And he's riding herd on a bunch of stallions that want to win and he doesn't know how to harness that power."

"And he was going to hand the reins over to you?" Jack asked.

"That was the agreement when I came on," Hill said. "But then last week Steve calls me into his office and says he's changed his mind. He doesn't feel like it's the right time, especially since his starting lineup is struggling with grades. He's got some hotshot freshman prospect coming up he wants to give some playing time to next season. Said we need to regroup and refocus on the future and let the current team phase out gracefully. Said none of them has what it takes to be a championship team or go any further than high school ball."

"And what'd you say to that?" Jack asked.

"I told him he was crazy," Hill said, taking a swig from the bottle. "I didn't even care that he said he wasn't retiring. But to basically give up on these boys when they've put everything into making the team they are today." He stopped and shook his head. "It doesn't even make sense. I think he was just afraid to go out on a loss and have someone take his spot who starts winning again. I can see how that would prick a man's pride and ego."

Jack hmmed sympathetically. "Is that when he told you your contract wasn't going to be renewed?"

"Ha," Hill said, getting worked up. "He didn't even have the balls to tell me then. I guess he worked it out with the school board and they'd be the ones to break the news. I tried calling him, and when he didn't answer my calls I showed up at his house. He's the one who hired me, so he should at least have the guts to fire me face-to-face."

"When was the last time you saw him?" Jack asked.

"Wednesday at school," Hill said. "Before the school board met. It was just a regular day. Nothing special. Then after I found out he'd stabbed me in the back I went out and got drunk. Called in sick on Thursday. When he didn't show up for school today I didn't think much of it. And then I started hearing the rumors that he'd killed himself. Maybe he felt guilty."

"Where were you this morning between six and eight o'clock?"

"I got to the weight room around seven to start letting the guys in who like to get an early workout," he said.

"Any other changes or upsets with staff or the players?" Jack asked.

"Oh, sure," Hill said. "Hargrove was about to shake up the whole apple cart. He wanted a whole new coaching staff. And he wanted to shake up his starting lineup. We've got a couple of guys with grade issues, but grades don't matter when you play like they do. But Hargrove was a stickler for grades. Said academics had to come first. Which is a great answer when you're talking to media and parents, but it doesn't mean crap when you're talking football. So take your pick."

Hill gestured wildly with his beer and I knew it wasn't his first. Probably not even his second even though he couldn't have been home from school too long.

"Between angry parents, coaches, and play-ers," Hill said, "I could think of a whole lot of reasons for Steve to want to end it all."

CHAPTER SIX

"First impressions?" Jack asked once we were back in the car.

"Definitely a disgruntled employee," I said. "Just like any story, there's threads of the truth in there colored by his own emotions. Mostly anger in his case. He's a guy on the edge. He's pretty much lost everything, and doesn't have much else to lose. But his alibi is easy to check out."

"Yeah, I know," Jack said. "Why is it so much easier when it's murder?"

"Because then it's someone else's fault," I said. "It's hard when those heroes get knocked down off their pedestals."

Jack looked at the time and said, "We've got time to grab dinner before we visit Cami Downey's roommate. Her name is Toby Wallace.

She's a law clerk as well and said they're in the middle of a case, so she's running late. I thought we'd do things her way before we show up with the forensic team and start going through the home."

"So diplomatic," I said. "She works for Judge Stevens too?"

"No," Jack said. "She works for Judge Mitchell. She's the one who filed the missing person report this morning."

"Cami has been dead at least a couple of days," I said. "She just now got concerned enough to file a report? She'd know there's no waiting period in Virginia to file for missing persons."

"I guess law clerks are busy and they don't see each other that often."

Jack pulled into the parking lot of the Silver Dollar Diner. I hadn't been there since I was a kid, but I always trusted cops to pick the best places to eat, so I didn't offer an opinion.

The Silver Dollar Diner was two old train cars that had been welded together and painted white with a red checkerboard trim. You could see straight through from one side to the other because of all the windows, and they were doing a brisk business considering the weather.

"Wow, this is a blast from the past," I said. "I don't remember the last time I was here."

"I do," Jack said. "Carly Martin's ninth birthday party. You were mad because you wanted to wear your vintage New Kids on the Block shirt and your mom made you wear a dress instead."

"Oh, yeah," I said. "I loved that shirt. Wish I still had it. They're back together again. I could wear it to their concert. I can't believe you remember that."

"There's not a lot about you I don't remember," he said, leaning over to kiss me softly. "You're the girl of my dreams, Dr. Graves."

"You keep that up and we'll end up skipping dinner," I said, feeling the warmth spread under my skin. "In fact, maybe we should skip dinner. There's a Holiday Inn right across the street."

"Are you crazy?" he asked, looking horrified. "We've already got a full moon and Friday the thirteenth. Do you know what you're like when you haven't been fed? I've only got so much manpower to spare."

"Hilarious," I said, getting out of the car.

"That's why you married me," he said, taking my hand.

"No, I definitely married you for your body. And your brains. And your body. If you play your cards right, I'll let you give me a refresher course on why I married you after you feed me."

"Very generous of you," Jack said, opening the door for me.

The smell of onion rings and grease assaulted my senses as soon as we walked in out of the wet, and my mouth started to water.

"I don't remember it being like this," I said, looking around at the fresh paint, retro memorabilia, and signed photographs of celebrities on the walls. The booths were red vinyl, the floors black-and-white checkerboard, and there was a soda fountain with stools that lined a long Formica bar.

"New owners," Jack said. "They renovated the place. I've been here a couple of times with the guys."

"How you keep that body I will never know," I said. "I can feel my hips expanding just breathing it in."

Jack squeezed my backside subtly and whispered, "One of the many reasons I married you."

"You are not helping me stay focused on getting back to work," I warned him. "You're not thinking ahead. What happens when we're both worked up to the point of self-combustion and then we have to stay the night at the sheriff's office because we can't make it back home?"

"Wow, you've already thought this out," he said. "Fascinating how your mind works."

"I'm a planner," I said. "In all things. Including where and when we can have sex. Because again, that body of yours is hard to resist. You're always just a hairsbreadth away from me jumping your bones at all times."

"The people would be shocked," Jack said, leading me to an empty booth.

"No they wouldn't," I said, winking saucily at him. "You're mine, I love you, and I can't keep my hands off you. All married people should be so blessed."

I wasn't the best at expressing my feelings. Jack was much better at it than I was, but I could tell he was touched by the way he squeezed my hand. It was just good timing that my phone rang so things didn't get too mushy.

"Graves," I answered, recognizing Lily's number on the screen.

"I just signed the death by sex guy in," she said. "Let's just say that rigor has most definitely set in and I am not looking forward to massaging that out. After today, I'm off food and sex. I have never seen an erection like that before. No wonder he's dead. Looks painful."

I winced in sympathy. Been there done that. Death puts a time stamp on the body. With the blood flowing to all Mr. Danforth's parts, he'd be frozen in time at that moment until rigor passed. But rigor lasted around twenty-four hours, which meant the only way to get rid of it to do the autopsy was to massage it out.

"It'll be tomorrow morning before I get to him," I said. "Maybe that'll give you the pardon you're looking for."

"I sure hope so," she said. "Though it is a great topic for a paper."

"Always look on the bright side," I said.

"In other news," she said, "I finished cleaning the skull fragments of Steve Hargrove. You're not going to believe this, but when I put the pieces together I found radiating fracture lines."

"You're kidding," I said, looking up at Jack. "That would explain the red flakes. That's a good find, Lily. Go ahead and run blood and urine samples on Mr. Danforth, and then wrap up whatever you need for the night and head out. I'm going to stop back by and take a look once we're done here."

"You don't have to tell me twice," she said, disconnecting the line.

"What?" Jack asked.

"Looks like we get a reprieve," I said. "Lily found radiating fracture lines on Steve Hargrove's skull. That along with the flakes I turned in to the lab are more than enough to determine it as a homicide. Blunt force trauma might not have been cause of death, but it was contributing. I'm still waiting on Cheney to come back with the lab results for the flakes."

"That's the best news I've had all day," he said. "Let's eat while we have a few seconds of peace."

That was easier said than done. Jack's phone went off the entire half hour we tried to shovel down food. The guy who'd been set on fire had died at the hospital, so Cole now had a homicide on his hands. Though it didn't look like it would be too terribly hard to solve as there'd been witnesses to the crime.

The calls for the night were just starting to come in. Several assaults, an attempted robbery at the convenience store, several calls of people trapped in rising water because they'd ignored the barricades that had been set out, and a guy threatening to jump off the Memorial Bridge into the Potomac.

"Let's go," I said. "I'm anxious to get back to the lab and look at Hargrove's skull. It's nothing short of a miracle that there was enough adjacent skull to piece together to see the fracturing."

"And maybe while we're at it we can figure

out who stabbed Cami Downey thirteen times and tossed her in the river."

It took us less time than I thought it would to navigate to the James Madison Bridge and King George Proper. The high waters weren't as bad around the university since they'd built in drainage systems, so we didn't have to make any detours.

"I'm not a parent," I said.

"Yet," Jack interjected.

"But I would never let my kid live in a place like this," I said. "No matter how old they were."

"Yeah," he said. "This is a hotspot area we keep on the radar. We've had trouble with vagrants and drugs being sold under the bridge. We raided a flophouse not too far from here."

"Geez," I said. "We've never had that kind of trouble in King George before."

"The price of progress," he said. "People move from DC to get out of DC, only they're bringing DC problems with them because they still want what they had in the city. The more developers move in, the more problems we'll have."

"Which is why we're not selling all the Lawson land."

"You do pay attention when I'm boring you with business stuff," he said, smiling.

Jack came from a long line of tobacco farmers. He'd inherited the land, properties, and a ridiculous amount of money from his grandparents when he'd turned twenty-five. Tobacco farming wasn't what it used to be, so as other farms had gone belly up, Jack had bought up their property so they wouldn't sell to developers. He'd started growing organic cotton and soybeans, and a couple of the pastures he used for grain fed chickens and cattle.

As far as the locals were concerned, Jack was a hero. He'd kept jobs intact and kept industries going that otherwise would've died out. Not to mention he'd kept the big city developers at bay. At least for now.

"Of course I do," I said. "You told me I needed to pay attention in case something happens to you and I end up running the Lawson estate. And then I told you I didn't want to talk about a future without you, so you promised I could have a dog. Which I still don't have, by the way, but I have lots of pictures on my Pinterest board."

"I think we got off track," Jack said, his smile

tight. "Let's see what we can find out about Cami Downey."

"I'm not going to forget about the dog," I said. "I want a big dog. But one that's soft and will sit in my lap."

"You've given this much more thought than I'm comfortable with," he said.

"A promise is a promise," I said. "You still have trauma from when Barbara died. And I still don't understand why you named your dog Barbara."

"Because I was five and I named her after my grandmother because she was my hero," he said. "And I don't want to talk about Barbara."

"Because you're still traumatized from her death. She was seventeen years old when she died. That's one hundred and nineteen in dog years. It was time for her to go."

"Maybe we could table this for later," he said.

"Fine, fine," I said. "I'm going to name our dog Sherlock. He'll be a great detective dog."

I saw Jack roll his eyes, but I decided to ignore it. I'd get my dog. Mostly because I'd never had one before. I hadn't had a regular childhood, and I'd always resented the fact that my parents would never let me have one. In hindsight, they probably hadn't wanted a dog to sniff out bodies they'd stashed in their underground bunker at the house or anything else that might lead the cops to their door.

The rain and gloom somehow made the area seem more sinister than it was in daylight. Street-lights flickered or were out completely, making it nearly impossible to see what lurked under the overpass. Jack turned his lights on and two cars that had been parked took off in opposite directions.

The city had made an attempt to revitalize the area since it was only a few blocks from campus, but so far the newly built conference center looked like a fish out of water among an old apartment complex, a bail bondsman, pawn shop, and a three-story building with grimy brick and bars on the first-floor windows.

Jack parked in front of the three-story build-ing, and the neon sign from the pawn shop flashed eerily over Jack's truck.

"This is where our victim lived?" I asked.

"I'm guessing they don't make much as law clerks, so the rent is cheap, and it's convenient to jump on the highway to get into DC quickly. But yeah, seems like there would be better options for two young women. I've got deputies and CSI on the way. They're about fifteen minutes out."

Jack knocked on a door with peeling green paint and a harried-looking man came to the door. He wore a blue button-down with his sleeves rolled up to the elbows and glasses. His hair was disheveled and there was what I presumed was a coffee stain down the front of his shirt.

Jack held up his badge before the guy could shut the door in our faces. "We're here to see Toby Wallace."

The guy stared at the badge a few seconds, his brow furrowed. "Oh, yeah," he said. "Come on in. She lives up on the third floor."

I looked around the entryway, noticing the stairs that were neatly tucked away in the corner. There was a big living area right in the center of the room with comfortable-looking couches and a fireplace that had candles in the firebox instead of wood. The interior of the house seemed to be in much better shape than the exterior and the furnishings were nice, if comfortably used. They had thick curtains over each of the barred windows.

"Do you live here?" Jack asked, looking around.

"Umm...yeah," he said. "What's this about?"

"Are you a lawyer too?"

"Yes," he said. "We're all law clerks. What do you want with Toby?"

"Do you have a name?"

"Will," he said. "Will Matthews."

Jack's expression was affable enough, but I could tell he was getting aggravated at having to pull answers out of Will.

"Do you know Cami Downey?" Jack asked.

"Of course," he said. "She lives here. She shares the third floor with Toby. Why?"

"Because Cami is dead," Jack said. "Maybe you could stop with the questions and start answering mine. How many people live here?"

"Wait a second," Will said, holding up a hand as if Jack were going to rush toward him. "What do you mean Cami is dead? How? When?"

"She was murdered," Jack said. "When was the last time you saw her?"

"I don't know," he said, looking agitated. "We all work crazy hours. Maybe two or three days ago. Maybe longer. But that's not uncommon depending on our workload. Am I a suspect? I'll schedule a formal inquiry at the police station and answer your questions there within reason. I'll let you know if I'll be representing myself or if I'll have a colleague stand in."

"You see, Will," Jack said, his voice nice and even. "What you're doing is making me think you have something to hide. When all I asked you was your name and how many people live here. Did you kill Cami Downey?"

"No, don't be absurd," he said, scoffing. "And I resent the implication."

"What I resent is you wasting my time," Jack said. "Now if you know anything about the law, which I'm starting to doubt, you'll know that we've got a team on the way to search this place because it's a murder. So I hope we don't find the reason your pupils are dilated to the size of saucers. Maybe a guy who has a cocaine problem isn't that far off from a guy who can commit murder."

The guy's fists balled up and his face turned an unhealthy shade of red. I was a little slow on the uptake, but it was clear now that the guy had been using. It wasn't uncommon in certain circles when you needed to pull all-nighters. There'd been a couple of doctors at the hospital while I was there who had a reputation for taking hits of cocaine to make it to end of shift.

"I do know the law," he said, leaning toward Jack, trying to intimidate him. "You've got to find probable cause to search the other apartments in this place. Good luck with that."

"The cocaine is probable cause, genius," Jack said.

Just when I thought the guy was going to charge at Jack, another man came out of a room on the opposite side of the living area.

"What the hell, Will," the man said, blocking Will from doing anything stupid. "Have you lost your mind? Do you want to go down for assaulting a police officer? Don't be stupid."

"It was provoked," Will said. "I want to file a grievance."

The other man turned to us and smiled with a lot of teeth. He was handsome and tanned and fit, with a Kennedyesque air about him. I disliked him instantly. I preferred guys like Will Matthews because you knew exactly where they stood.

"John Tippin," the man with the smile said, holding out a hand to Jack. "I'll apologize for my friend. He's been under a lot of stress lately. He clerks for Judge Clark. The rest of us have it easy compared to Will. No one can kick your ass quite like Judge Clark."

Jack played along and shook John's hand, letting the guy talk.

"Is there something I can help you fine officers with?" John asked.

"I'm Sheriff Lawson," Jack said. "This is Dr. Graves. She's the coroner for the county. Cami Downey was murdered. We need anyone who lives in the house to come downstairs and answer a few questions."

John's tan paled and his arm dropped and went limp at his side. "Cami?" he asked. "You've got to be wrong. She's just working. Sometimes she stays at the hotel down the street from the courthouse if it gets too late. I'll call her cell. You'll see. It's not her."

"I'm sorry for your loss," Jack said. "She's been identified through both prints and dental records. Can you get her roommate for me? And anyone else in the house."

John nodded, his motions jerky, and I didn't think he was faking his reaction. Cami's death had hit him hard.

"I'll go get her," Will said, squeezing John's shoulder and narrowing his eyes at Jack.

"I think I need a drink," John said, moving over to a sideboard that had been cleverly turned into a bar. He poured three fingers of whiskey and took a deep drink, and then he dropped down into the chair closest to the fireplace, as if Jack and I weren't there at all.

"What was your relationship with Ms. Downey?" Jack asked. We sat on the love seat across from John, but he never looked at us.

"We were friends," he said, looking into his drink. "Sometimes lovers. But it was nothing serious. Mostly friends."

"Mostly?" Jack asked. "You guys have a fight?"

John smiled, this one more real than the polished one he'd given us before. "We're attorneys. Or at least, most of us are. We're always arguing about something. But no, Cami and I were more friends than lovers. It's just that in our line of work there's not a lot of time for dating or relationships, so when one of us had a need it was convenient."

"How many people live in this building?" I asked.

"There's six of us," John said. "Two on each floor. Will and I share the bottom floor, and there's also a common kitchen and living space down here. Thea and Kevin bunk on the second level. And then Toby and Cami on the third floor. But everyone has their own apartment suite. It's a great setup."

"And did you or Cami have a sexual relationship with anyone else in the house?" Jack asked.

"I don't think Cami did," he said. "She was really focused on her career. I used to hook up with Toby when we were in law school, but that's been a couple of years. And I hooked up with Thea once, but she got weird about it so I decided once was enough. Thea's kind of clingy. She's big on relationships." John gave us air quotes when he said *relationships*.

"You were all in law school together?" Jack asked.

"Yeah," he said. "Went in together and graduated together. Top of our class. Which is why we all got judge clerkships, and we started hanging together. Well, plus Kevin's dad is in Congress so that's why he's a clerk. But I don't think he really wants to be. Every one of us has taken and passed the bar exam except for Thea. And she's due to take it in a couple of weeks. I don't understand. What happened to Cami?"

"That's what we're trying to find out," Jack said as Will and a young woman came down the stairs.

Jack and I stood as introductions were made. Toby Wallace was more delicate than I expected her to be. I knew law clerks had to have a thick skin and a bulldog determination. Those were coveted positions that didn't come easily.

She was slight of build and slender, with strawberry-blond hair and a smattering of freckles across her nose. She was pretty in a girl-next-door kind of way, but she was someone who'd blend in as nondescript if in a room of other attractive people. There were dark circles under her eyes and she twisted the silver ring on her finger nervously. She stood just in front of Will, near the stairs.

"Did you find Cami?" she asked. "Is she okay? Sometimes I don't see her for a couple of days, but I knew when I woke up this morning and didn't see her that something wasn't right."

"Where are the other two roommates?" Jack asked. "Kevin and Thea, I think you said."

"Thea works at the Mad King a few nights a week to make extra money," Will said. "She went to law school on student loans. Kevin usually hangs out there with her because he's an alcoholic and she gives him free drinks."

"What happened to Cami?" John asked, knocking back the rest of his drink.

"Her body washed up this morning in Gambo Creek," Jack said. "We estimate time of death somewhere between thirty and sixty hours ago. When was the last time any of you saw her?"

Toby's face paled at the news and a tear snaked down her cheek. "Umm," she said, twisting her ring more.

"Sit down, Toby," Will said, pushing her gently onto the other sofa. "You look like you're about to fall over."

"Tuesday," she said. "Cami wasn't feeling great, so she stayed home to work. I got home at a fairly reasonable hour, so we ordered Chinese food around seven thirty and then we both went back to work. Cami felt better after dinner and said she needed to go into the office for some files, so she showered and got dressed, and then she left."

"She didn't come home that night?" Jack asked.

"I...I'm not sure," Toby said, shrugging. "We all keep weird hours. I had a splitting headache, so I took something and went to bed. And then I got up about six and got ready for work like usual."

"How does Cami get to work?" I asked.

"Sometimes we carpool," she said. "John and Kevin both have cars so we ride with them in the mornings. And then in the evenings we use rideshare. It's cheaper than having a car. At least for now. Besides, John's car has been broken into several times since we've lived here. It's not a great neighborhood."

"Did Cami pack a bag to take with her?" Jack asked. "Anyone she would've stayed the night with?"

Toby looked at John quickly and then back down at her hands, making it clear that his sexual relationship with Cami was known among the others.

"No," she said. "She didn't have anything with her but her purse. She just said she'd be back in a couple of hours with the files she needed."

"What about you guys," Jack said. "Did you see her leave or come back home?"

"I was out that night," John said. "I was at a dinner at Le Chez with Judge Mitchell and several other attorneys who have judgeship appointments coming. I didn't come home until well after midnight."

"You clerk for Judge Mitchell too?" Jack asked, looking between him and Toby.

As soon as Jack asked the question, Toby's shoulders tensed and she stopped twisting the ring on her finger.

"I wasn't invited," Toby said, arching a brow. "Mitchell likes the boys' club and he likes to let his female clerks do all the work."

"You know that's not true, Toby," John said. "We all work hard. But Judge Mitchell knows my goal is to end up on the bench. And that's a politics game that you're not willing to play. He's just helping me network and meet the right people."

"Sure," Toby said, rolling her eyes.

It sounded like a familiar argument.

"What about you?" Jack asked Will.

"I was here," he said. "But I was in my room. I had a friend stay late. She left about two in the morning, and then I went to sleep."

"What's her name?"

Will hesitated for a second. "Is that important?"

"I wouldn't ask if it wasn't," Jack said. "We can move much faster and catch whoever did this if we can verify all of your whereabouts."

Will nodded. "Helena Rosenberg."

"We'll need to contact her for confirmation," Jack said.

"God, Will," John said, looking at him with disgust. "Helena? Are you stupid? Do you know who her father is? Do you even want a career?"

"Shut up, John," Will said, standing and moving over to the bar to pour himself a drink. His hands shook, and I knew he'd much rather have a hit of whatever had him flying high when we'd arrived.

"Who's Helena Rosenberg?" Jack asked. "Just so we know what we're dealing with."

"Richard Rosenberg's daughter," John said, still looking at Will like he'd grown a horn out of the middle of his forehead. "Like, Supreme Court Justice Richard Rosenberg."

Jack was an excellent poker player and his face displayed none of the annoyance I'm sure he was feeling at that bit of information.

There was a knock on the front door, and Jack looked down at his watch. "That'll be the rest of the team," Jack said. "We'll need all of you to stay confined in this area for the moment. I'm sure you all know the drill. Dr. Graves and I will start upstairs in Cami's room."

"Do you have a warrant?" Will asked, knocking back three fingers of whiskey in one gulp.

"We've already been over this, Will," Jack said, shaking his head. "I don't need one for any common areas. This is an active murder investigation. This is Cami Downey's place of residence. We're going to search it. Because someone stabbed her thirteen times and tossed her in the creek."

Toby gasped and put her hands over her mouth. "Oh, my God. I can't believe this is real. This can't be real."

Jack went to let the CSI team in and gave instructions on where to start. Will kept eyeing the door to his apartment, and I wondered if it was because he was looking for a fix or because he had something to hide.

CHAPTER SEVEN

JACK AND I LEFT THE DEPUTIES DOWNSTAIRS TO keep watch over the roommates, and we left CSI to do their thing so we could head upstairs to Cami's apartment. We made it to the second landing and looked around.

"Kevin's and Thea's apartments," Jack said.

There was a door on each side, but no common areas like downstairs.

"I wonder how everyone really gets along," I said. "There's tension. Between John and Thea because of the favoritism with Judge Mitchell. Maybe John and Kevin. He sounded a little resentful when he insinuated that Kevin got his clerkship because of his father's position in Congress."

"Yeah, not to mention John has slept with all

three of the women in this house," Jack said. "That would make things uncomfortable under normal circumstances."

"The common denominator with the tension seems to be John," I said.

"I noticed that," Jack said. "Plus there's Will's drug problem, which probably makes things volatile."

"And don't forget Kevin is an alcoholic and Thea is needy," I said.

"John was full of useful information on his roommates, wasn't he?"

I handed Jack a pair of gloves and put on my own, and he tested the doorknob. It opened with a squeak of hinges and we went inside.

"Unlocked," Jack said. "I wonder if that's the norm."

"Big space," I said, looking around. "Tidy. Feminine."

The room was more like an efficiency apartment. A corner of the room had a table and two chairs, a sink and a dorm refrigerator. The table was stacked with files and other papers, and there was a pair of reading glasses on top. There was a purse on the kitchen chair.

"Purse," I said, moving over to it. "Toby said Cami had it with her when she left to go to the office."

"Looks like she made it back," Jack said. "Or maybe she never left at all."

"No wallet or cell phone inside," I said. "It's empty. Maybe she was using a different purse."

In the middle of the room was a small chintz sofa with a faded rose pattern and a coffee table. There was a TV mounted to the wall and a table beneath it with candles and pictures of smiling people in frames.

"None of these pictures have her roommates in them," I said, picking up one of the frames.

"Interesting," Jack said. "These kids have spent a lot of time together. College, law school, same workplace, and then they're living together on top of it."

"Maybe they're sick of each other," I said, putting down the picture. "I know I'd get tired of them."

Jack snorted out a laugh. "Tell me how you really feel."

I smiled cheekily. "I just did. I don't like them at all. Even Toby had something about her that put me off, and she seemed to genuinely be upset over Cami's death."

"It's because they're attorneys," Jack said. "You never like attorneys."

"That's because in our line of work attorneys tend to make our lives and jobs harder."

"Yes, but in our other line of work that includes our properties and investments, our attorneys are quite likeable and have our best interest at heart."

"Only because our best interest lines their pockets," I said skeptically.

I ran my finger over the top of the sofa table and saw the dust on my fingers. On the far side of the room was a queen-size bed with a pale peach duvet and a lot of fussy pillows. The bed wasn't made. There was a single nightstand with a lamp, and a door that led to a small bathroom. The floors were wood and scarred, but she'd scattered rugs over the worst of it.

"So we've got a twenty-four-year-old woman who's got a prestigious job as a law clerk for a federal judge," I said. "She's got no vehicle, and this place screams of good taste but not a lot of money. She's been dead too long for any contents to be in her stomach, so I can't verify that Chinese food was her last meal. The roommate said Cami showered and changed clothes to go into the office, but we found her in sexy lingerie. And we don't have the murder weapon or the location she was killed."

"That pretty much sums it up," Jack said, going through the trash. "No signs of Chinese food up here. Maybe they ate down in the kitchen. Only thing in the trash is coffee grounds and some tissues. We'll let CSI go through that in case they can get DNA."

"These candles are all guttered out," I said, looking into the glass jars beneath the TV. "She either left them all burning when she left, or she came back home that night and changed into something sexy and lit candles. She could have been watching a *Bridgerton* marathon or she could have been expecting company."

"Women are so strange," Jack said, shaking his head. "The bed has been slept in. Both pillows have a head indentation."

"There was no seminal fluid or secretions when I did the autopsy, but none were really expected with the submersion in water. No vaginal tearing. If she had sex it was consensual. But her underwear was on and intact when we found her. That doesn't explain where or how she got the contusion along her jaw. It was definitely perimortem."

"Maybe they had a fight after they had sex," Jack said. "Maybe she put her underwear and the night thing back on. Wonder if she has a robe or something. Usually when there's a fight after intimacy women tend to cover up. Things got heated and he struck her. A hard enough blow could have knocked her out."

"Could be," I said, running the scenario through my head. "Or maybe she brings someone new back to her place and old John downstairs isn't too happy about it. When the new lover leaves he and Cami get into it. He knocks her out and kills her."

Jack grunted. "I like that one. I don't like that guy. We'll see if CSI can light up some luminol anywhere in the house. We need a location where she was killed."

"The other scenario is that she never came back that night at all," I said. "Toby said she had her purse. Maybe she shoved her sexy nightie in her bag and went to the office to meet her lover. Maybe she didn't want to bring a new lover home and have him bump into John."

"Except her body ended up back in King George," Jack said. "So if she did go into DC she made it back into the county alive. Seems like too much trouble for someone to kill her there and then bring her body back across state lines and dump her in the creek. It'll be easy enough to check and see if she actually went into the office. All of the judges' staff members are given swipe cards. It shouldn't be hard to confirm. We can check with the rideshare companies too. The question is where did she go when she came back?"

"Maybe we're making it too complicated," I said. "John is her usual bed buddy. Maybe he's the second pillow."

"Without the crime scene location and the murder weapon we're up a creek without a paddle on this one."

"We might be able to get some hair or skin cells from the other pillow," I said, opening the nightstand drawer. "Usual stuff in here. Box of condoms that's half full. Some toys. A couple of pens and a .38 special."

"Loaded?" Jack asked.

"Six bullets all accounted for," I said, handing it to him. "A box of bullets underneath it."

"We'll test it anyway to see if it's been fired recently," he said.

We moved into the bathroom. "All her toiletries are still here," I said. "And makeup. Things she'd normally pack if she was staying overnight somewhere else."

"We'll track down Thea and Kevin and get their alibis," Jack said, making his way back into the room. "We'll need to look at Cami's cases too and see if she was working anything that might be dangerous or controversial."

"But you don't think so," I said.

"No. Being stabbed thirteen times is personal."

"Very," I said, agreeing. "Some of those stab wounds were deep. That kind of rage doesn't normally come from a street criminal hoping to score some cash for drugs. We just need to find out what could make someone elicit that kind of rage."

"We need to talk to all of them individually," Jack said. "Tomorrow. Put them on ice for a bit. They're not going to like being displaced."

We closed Cami's door behind us and then went back downstairs to join the others. Cami's roommates were all where we'd left them in the living area, but they stopped talking when they noticed us.

Jack looked at Toby and asked, "Where did you and Cami eat dinner?"

"Down here," she said blankly. "In the kitchen."

"You said you ate around seven thirty?" Jack asked.

"That's when I called it in," she said. "I remember because the menu for the Chinese place is on the bulletin board next to the clock in the kitchen. The delivery guy got here around eight o'clock."

"And what time did Cami leave to go to the office?"

Toby looked off in the distance, trying to recall. "It was probably close to ten," she said.

"That's not unusual to go in that late?" he asked.

"Not really," Toby said. "I've gone in at three in the morning before when I realized I left papers I needed at the office. It isn't unusual to work all-nighters. Cami and I sat down here talking for a while after dinner. And then she got a text on her phone and she kind of rolled her eyes and said she was going to have a late night, and that she had to go pick up some files from the office."

"How long does it take to get from here to the office?" Jack asked.

"Right at an hour fifteen when there's no traffic," Toby said. "The reason we live in this dump is because it's an easy drive into the city and it's dirt cheap."

"Hey," John said. "This place is a good investment. And you hardly have to pay anything."

"It's a good investment for you," Toby said, rolling her eyes. "You own the building and I'm sure you'll sell it for a fortune. The rest of us risk our lives every time we leave the house." She must have realized what she said because she gasped and covered her hands with her mouth.

"Oh, God. That's what happened to Cami. It could have been any of us."

"It looked like Cami had an overnight guest when we were looking through her room," Jack said, looking at John. "When was the last time you slept with Cami?"

John wiped his hand over his face. "This is surreal. I stayed at her place Monday night. I was gone to dinner on Tuesday night, like I told you before. I drove Toby and Will to work Tuesday morning and brought a change of clothes with me for dinner. Toby said Cami was sick, so I didn't see her all day. You can check my alibi easily enough."

"We will," Jack said.

"Sheriff." Phil Olson was one of the crime scene investigators, and he stuck his head out of the kitchen to get Jack's attention.

We followed him into a spacious commercial kitchen that had been newly renovated with stainless-steel appliances, black countertops, and black-painted cabinets with modern silver pulls on each door. It was sleek and expensive and modern, and it didn't go with the rest of the house at all. If I had to guess, I'd say John's apartment looked a lot like this kitchen.

"What's up, Olson?" Jack said.

"We've got a knife missing from the block,"

he said. "That's a nice set. Expensive. Knife that's missing is about nine inches with a serrated blade. It would match the other steak knives."

"Perfect," Jack said.

Three sets of eyes looked at us curiously when we came back in the living area. "Are there any dishes in the dishwasher?" he asked.

"No," Will said. "I unloaded it when I got home from work. It was my night for kitchen duty."

"Whose night was it Tuesday night?" Jack asked.

They all looked at each other. "It was Cami's," John said.

Jack looked down at his phone, and I could see from the corner of my eye he was requesting a warrant for the entire house. The knife missing from the block meant we had probable cause to search every room. And because the knife was small, it meant we'd be able to look in every nook and cranny.

"You all need to vacate the premises until we clear it for you to reenter," Jack finally told them. "A deputy will escort each of you out. You can't take anything with out. Leave your laptops, files, and vehicles. The whole premises is on lock down."

"Wait a minute," John said, getting to his feet.

"You will need a warrant to start searching our apartments. We're entitled to privacy. And until you get that warrant you can't confiscate any of our personal belongings."

"Good thing they're not being confiscated," Jack said, smiling. "This is an active crime scene investigation. We have the authority to shut this entire building down, and that's what we're doing. We will not enter your private domiciles until I have the warrant in hand, but you won't be entering them either. Don't leave town. You'll all be contacted to come down to the station for an informal interview. I suggest you cooperate so you can all come home sooner."

Will looked toward his bedroom door again, the color draining from his face. If I were forensics, I'd start with his room.

———

Jack and I did a pass around the building where Cami Downey lived, hoping we'd get lucky and find an alley full of blood and a knife. We found nothing but a dumpster, two abandoned cars, and a broken chain-link fence. There was a closed garage where I assumed John and Kevin kept their vehicles. Jack got one of the deputies to open up the garage so we could take a look inside.

"The BMW must be John's," I said. "No wonder it's been broken into. He's kind of asking for it in this neighborhood."

"That's a privileged kid," Jack said. "He owns this building, fancy car, political aspirations and he already has the connections to get him where he's going."

"Maybe Cami was upsetting the apple cart, or she knew something that could upset his future plans," I said.

"Yeah, I like him for it," Jack said. "Just for the reason that we've known a hundred guys like that, and they never become better people as they get older."

Jack shined his flashlight inside the car, but there was nothing but white leather seats and a pair of sunglasses sitting on the console.

"We'll pop the trunk and make sure he's not hiding anything obvious," he said. "And then we'll tow the car to the station so the team can go through everything with a fine-tooth comb. Someone had to have transported her the night she died to dump her in the creek."

The deputy handed Jack the keys to the car and he popped the trunk.

"Nothing," I said, looking inside. "Not even a tire iron or a scrap of paper."

"Yes, almost like new," Jack said, slamming the trunk closed. "If anyone can find something, Cheney can. I'll make sure she gets assigned to this one. We can't do anything outside tonight. I'll have a team come back first thing in the morning to get started on the perimeter and to start doing door-to-doors. And I'll have another team start searching up and down the creek. It's only a four-mile stretch."

"How far are we from Gambo Creek?" I asked, getting back into Jack's truck.

"About half a mile east," he said. "Maybe less. A couple of minutes' drive from here."

"Gambo Creek starts in Bloody Mary, and like you said, it's only about four miles long until it dumps into the Potomac. We found her about two miles as the creek runs down from here, and we can presume she'd been in the water since early Wednesday morning."

"It rained Tuesday and into Wednesday," Jack said. "It wasn't like today, but it was a steady mist all day. It would've been a good time to dump a body. Low visibility. And a lot of Gambo Creek goes through uninhabited land like where we found her. Lots of trees and shrubs for cover."

"You'd have to know the area pretty well to

dump her in one of the uninhabited areas," I said, adjusting the heater and turning it on high so I could dry out a little bit. "That would make it more probable that her killer was someone local."

"So," Jack said, starting the truck and turning on the wipers. "We've narrowed it down that we think Cami Downey was murdered somewhere in King George County." He blew out a breath of frustration. "I'm really starting to hate this rain."

He pulled over underneath the bridge and was scrolling in his phone. "We need to go round up Thea and Kevin and talk to them before the others get a chance to talk to them."

I listened as he made a call and asked if Thea Miller was bartending.

"She's on shift until two o'clock," Jack said. "Unless you need to get back to the funeral home."

"It'll keep," I said. "It doesn't look like we'll be going home tonight anyway."

"Good thing we don't have a dog," he said.

"Sherlock would have been riding shotgun all day," I said. "He'd probably already have this case solved."

"Gosh," Jack said sarcastically. "It's too bad Sherlock is just a figment of your imagination. We could really use his help right now."

The Mad King was a block off campus, and it was crowded on a Friday night, even though most of the cars parked on the street had water halfway up their tires. There was a twenty-four-hour breakfast place across the street and a few other fast-food restaurants scattered about. All of it was close enough for students to walk from campus or the apartments close by, though why anyone would want to get out and walk in this was beyond my imagination. Maybe twenty-one-year-olds didn't feel the rain as long as there was the promise of booze at the end of the rainbow. It had been a long time since I'd been that age, but I knew without a doubt I'd been full of bad decisions and invincibility.

My head bumped against the window as Jack drove onto the sidewalk in front of the bar and flipped his lights on.

"Front door service," I said. "I like this part of being married to a cop."

I used my jacket to cover my head from the rain for the short trip inside.

The Mad King was like any other college bar. There were KGU flags hung on the walls and over the bar, basketball and football jerseys in glass-front frames, and televisions in every corner and along the walls. Every TV was playing the KGU basketball game, which had apparently gone into overtime because everyone was screaming and yelling, wearing their red-and-gold shirts proudly.

We maneuvered our way past pub tables and bodies toward the end of the bar. There was only one female bartender, so I assumed I was looking at Thea Miller.

She was attractive in a nerdy kind of way. Her dark hair was pulled up in a ponytail and tied with a scarf, and she wore black-framed glasses. Her face was thin and her lips painted bright red. Her uniform was similar to the male bartenders with a black pinstripe vest, white button-down shirt and black slacks. Her fingers were long and slender and she wore silver rings on the middle fingers of each hand. She was checking a couple of IDs while pouring two drafts.

Each of the barstools was full, but Jack showed his badge and a group of three guys took their beers and made themselves scarce. I wondered how close she was checking the IDs because they all looked very young. Of course, the older I got the more everyone started to look very young.

"Thea Miller?" Jack asked.

"Who wants to know?" the guy to my right said.

"You must be Kevin," Jack said, smiling with a lot of teeth.

"Like I said, who wants to know? I'm trying to watch the game."

It was clear this guy was already well on his way to drunk, and I was starting to see an unhealthy pattern emerging with the roommates.

"We're investigating the murder of Cami Downey," Jack said. "And you're both going to want to answer questions without the hassle because I'm feeling kind of mean, and I've already had to talk with your roommates and deal with the lawyer stuff. I don't care that you're a lawyer. I care that a girl was murdered. Just like you should because it's what decent people do."

Kevin was tall and thin through the face with defined cheekbones and arresting blue eyes. His hair was dark brown and unruly, longer over the collar and ears than his two male roommates. He didn't look like an attorney. He looked like a rich kid who had too much time and money on his hands. I was starting to see a pattern there too.

"Wait a second," Thea said, narrowing her eyes and wiping wet rings off the bar. "You're saying Cami is dead? Come on." She scoffed and started making another drink. "Who are you really? Did John put you up to this?"

"What kind of friends do you have that they'd play a joke on you like that?" I asked.

"You'd have to know John," she said, still looking skeptical.

"We've met him," I told her. "I'm Dr. Graves. I performed Cami's autopsy. She was stabbed thirteen times and dumped in Gambo Creek. You guys don't live too far from Gambo Creek."

Kevin froze and his grip tightened on his beer. "If Cami is dead we didn't have anything to do with it. It sucks, but it sounds like you're looking for a scapegoat so you can solve a case. And it's not us."

"Not a scapegoat," Jack said slowly. "A murderer. We're looking for a murderer. So where were you Tuesday night into early Wednesday morning?"

Keven saluted Jack with his bottle of beer. "Right here," he said. "Thea was working."

"And you always follow Thea to work?" Jack asked.

"When I can," Kevin said. "Keeps the guys from hassling her."

"You get a lot of guys hassling you?" I asked her.

"Not really," she said, rolling her eyes. "Harmless stuff."

"What time did you get off?" Jack asked Thea.

"Two," she said.

"And then where did you go?" Jack asked.

"Home," she said. "I mean, this is King George. It's not like there's an exciting nightlife. Besides, I had to be at the library early Wednesday morning to study, so we went straight home from here."

"What time did you get there?" Jack asked.

"I don't know," she said, shrugging. "By the time I closed everything down here it was probably half past two. Me and Robbie were the closers and we left together. So maybe fifteen minutes after that? It's not a long drive."

"Did you see any of your roommates when you got home?"

"Yeah, actually," Thea said, her brow furrowing. "We saw Cami. She was in the kitchen. Said she was having trouble sleeping and was out of wine in her apartment. We told her good night and headed upstairs."

"She seem bothered by anything?" Jack asked. "Upset?"

"No," Thea said. "She was in a good mood. John always keeps good wine on hand. He's kind of a snob about it. But she was holding one of his favorite reds."

"How was she dressed?" I asked.

"Why does that matter?" Kevin asked belligerently. "Perv."

"Thea?" Jack asked, ignoring Kevin.

"Umm...she was in her robe," she said, glancing at Kevin. "Like usual. She was always wearing that thing around the house. It's a white fluffy robe. Makes her look like a marshmallow. It was just a regular night. Nothing special. We live together, but we all lead our own lives. I'm sorry she's dead. Really, I am. I'm not callous to the fact that we live in a terrible neighborhood and it could have been me or Toby instead of Cami. We've asked John to put in cameras for safety, but he says he's not ready for that expense yet. Kevin and I have been talking about moving out and getting our own place anyway. Once I pass the bar my salary will increase and we'll be able to afford something."

"Geez, Thea," Kevin said, scowling. "Why don't you give them your life story while you're at it. How are you going to pass the bar when you haven't even learned to keep your mouth shut."

"Shut up, Kevin," Thea said. "You're drunk."

"Why do you need to keep your mouth shut?" Jack asked, leaning in close to Kevin. "Do you have something to say?"

"Get out of my face, man," Kevin said. "Only thing I feel bad about is that Cami's murderer will never get caught because she was murdered in this dumb hick town and you're a dumb hick cop."

Jack moved in even closer, but didn't touch him. "Did you kill her? A drunk like you won't be able to hide his stupidity. Killers are usually stupid you know. They always leave something behind. We'll find it."

"I said get out of my face," Kevin said, pushing back from his stool and swinging at Jack. His fist glanced off Jack's chin.

Jack smiled and said, "I was hoping you'd do that." And then he twisted Kevin's fingers and jerked his arm behind his back, pushing his head down on the bar.

"Geez, Kevin," Thea said sweetly. "How'd you ever pass the bar? You should know better than to assault a cop."

We were drawing the attention of several people who'd lost interest in the game. Jack put handcuffs on Kevin.

"It won't stick," I said. "And it'll be paperwork. And a headache from his father."

Jack shrugged. "That's the reason it's worth it. Pricks like this are pricks because no one calls them on it."

"This is entrapment," Kevin yelled, struggling against Jack. "I'm going to sue the hell out of you.

My father will buy and sell you. If you don't end up having an accident of your own. You don't know who you're messing with."

"Wow, that sounded like a threat," Jack said. "And I don't really care who your father is. Like I said, we're in the middle of a murder investigation, and I just don't like you. Maybe a night in a cell with a couple of other drunks will change your disposition."

Jack called in for a black-and-white to meet him out front so Kevin could be transported.

"By the way," Jack said to Thea. "The house is part of the crime scene. You'll need to find other accommodations until we're done with the search. The house is off limits. Does Kevin have his vehicle?"

"Yeah, it's parked around back," she said, frowning.

"We'll impound it to the station," he said. "A deputy will take you to a hotel or wherever you'll be staying for the time being."

"But I've got to work," she said. "And study. Kevin is my ride."

"Seems like you could do better," I said. "Good luck on the bar exam."

The rain hadn't stopped and we had at least two unsolved murders on our plate, but arresting Kevin had cheered Jack up immensely.

CHAPTER EIGHT

Jack dropped me off at the funeral home and left so he could be there when Kevin was processed. I knew Jack was frustrated and tired, but he'd work through the night to find out the truth of what had happened to Cami Downey. The problem was, we didn't have a lot to work on and time was already against us. The longer someone was dead, the harder it was to find their killer.

We already knew the creek was too high for us to get home tonight, so Jack decided to go back to his office to set up murder boards for Cami. And if I confirmed the fracturing in Coach Hargrove's skull, Jack would have reason to set up a murder board for him as well.

I'd already had enough coffee for the day so I grabbed a bottle of water, popped a couple of ibuprofen, and headed downstairs to the lab. I liked the funeral home the best when it was quiet and empty. It had never bothered me to be alone with the dead.

Lily had left everything nice and tidy, and I found all her notes on my desk and the samples I'd asked her to take from Rooney Danforth, our death by sex victim. I could run his labs and wait for the tox screen results while I took a look at Coach Hargrove.

I walked into the refrigeration unit, bypassing Coach Hargrove's body and moving toward the tray of skull fragments on the shelf. I carried it out and then placed everything carefully on my exam table, using the under lights beneath the table so I could see every mark and crevice.

It didn't take me long to confirm Lily's discovery. I didn't have an entire skull to work with, and only a small fraction of the parietal and occipital, but at the edge of one of the fragments was fracturing that looked like a small spiderweb. I double-checked to make sure it hadn't been caused by the buckshot, but bullets and buckshot left a very distinct marking on bone. This kind of fracturing could only be caused by one thing. Blunt force trauma.

I took pictures and documented everything, and then I updated Hargrove's file with my official ruling before putting everything back in the refrigeration unit.

And then I saw the tox results for Mr. Danforth. "Well, well, well," I said, immediately running the test again for confirmation.

His autopsy was set for the next morning, but the evidence in his bloodstream was pretty damning. He had six times the amount of sildenafil in his system that a regular dose of erectile dysfunction medicine would contain. And contrary to popular belief, a man could take too much. Cardiac arrest was only one of the problems an overdose could pose. I couldn't think of a man alive who would willingly take six times the amount on purpose.

The second tox screen came back the same as the first, and I left the file out on my desk so it would be ready once I started the autopsy the next morning. I cleaned up and then ran back upstairs full of more energy than I should have been considering it had already been a sixteen-hour day.

I grabbed a change of clothes from my office and shoved them in my bag, and I pulled on my parka but didn't bother zipping it up. I was still damp from the day. The Suburban was parked under the carport where Lily had left it.

It took me longer than usual to get to the sheriff's office. The bars were all open and filled to the brim, and every parking space in the Towne Square was taken. I was glad I was no longer on duty in the ER. Nights like this made for great stories, but terrible realities, and everyone working tonight would go home dead on their feet.

I finally lost patience looking for a parking space and parked in a tow-away zone. All the cops knew my vehicle, and I was willing to take the chance it would still be here when I was ready to leave.

There was a break in the clouds long enough for me to see the cause of all the bedlam. The full moon shone bright for a few seconds, and then the clouds rolled back in front of it. I heard a shriek of laughter as I got out of the car, and then I fell back against the door as a group of college-age kids ran down the street. The leader of the pack was totally naked and he leapt across the lawn of the courthouse like a gazelle.

Chasing streakers was outside of my pay grade, thank God, so I hitched my bag up, ran across the street, and went through the front door of the sheriff's office. There was a new sergeant at the front desk, but he was just as swamped as Hill had been earlier. I was let in through the side door and I couldn't get back to Jack's office fast enough.

His door was closed, but his blinds were open and I could see him sitting on the edge of his desk, staring at a wall of whiteboards. I knocked once and then let myself in, closing the door quickly behind me.

"I'm peopled out," I said. "When did all these people move to King George County? I think they're all gathered in the Towne Square tonight. I saw someone leaving the bar with a baby in a car seat. And I just passed a streaker on my way in."

"Yeah, we've been getting calls about him," Jack said absentmindedly. "Apparently, he's very fast and has covered a lot of ground. I've got uniforms looking for him."

"He was definitely fast," I agreed. "I guess youth has its advantages. What's up with you?"

"Just getting everything laid out on the boards," he said. "The knife missing from the kitchen is nine inches long. Part of a set. Serrated blade."

"Yeah, that fits with the wounds in her chest and abdomen," I said. "They find anything else?"

"Cami's robe was hanging in her closet," Jack

said. "The one Thea and Kevin saw her in. And there was another robe that matched her nightie kicked under the bed. It was torn. There was no bottle of wine or glasses up in her apartment. No empty bottles in the trash can."

"It's been a couple of days," I said. "Maybe they'll find something in the dumpster out back."

"One of those kids killed that girl," he said. "Murder weapon originated in the house, but we don't have it. And we wouldn't have a body if she'd floated down the creek and into the Potomac like she was supposed to. We also don't have the location of the murder. With that many stab wounds there has to be blood somewhere. I'm getting warrants to check vehicles and the roommates' apartments."

"Has next of kin been notified?" I asked.

"Cami's not a local girl," he said. "She's from Florida. She's got parents and two younger brothers. Looks like a nice family. She was the first to graduate from college and then law school. They're devastated.

"We're doing deep background checks on each of the roommates. Something doesn't feel right about the events of that night. Still waiting to hear whether or not she went into the office, and I've not gotten a response from Judge Wallner on the warrant."

"It's late," I said. "I'm sure he'll get to it in the morning. Whatever Cami was working on was important enough that she got dressed and went into the city for those files, so we can't rule out a case as the reason for her death. But it's contradictory."

"In what way?" Jack asked.

"If I'm home and I forgot something at work," I said. "I'm not going to shower and put on fresh clothes. I'm going to toss whatever is closest on and make a quick run and be back as soon as I can. And when I get back, I sure as heck am not going to open a bottle of wine. I wouldn't get anything done."

"Which begs the questions," Jack said. "What was she working on? And *who* was she working with? We find her in sexy lingerie and it was obvious two people had been in that bed. Do you buy John's story about him being with her the night before?"

"Maybe he was," I said, shrugging. "But you saw how neat that apartment was. Someone who keeps house like that probably makes their bed every day. So if John was with her Monday night and not Tuesday night, then who was with her the night she died?"

"Well, according to Thea and Kevin she was still alive around 3 a.m. Wednesday morning."

"Yes, and she was in a good mood and getting wine," I said. "So maybe someone was still upstairs at that time, and the wine was for both of them. She's already dressed in her night-clothes. Just threw her robe on to run downstairs. Kevin and Thea go up to their floor. Will said he let his lady friend out around two in the morning."

"There's a lot of in-and-out activity at that time of the morning," Jack said. "John got home from the dinner with Judge Mitchell after midnight. Maybe he went upstairs to do a repeat of the night before with Cami and she was with someone else. Or maybe he lied and he was the other person in her bed."

He rubbed a hand over his face and then pressed his fingers against his eyes.

"I want to talk to Toby and Thea again," Jack said. "Will is a self-absorbed cokehead, and John will do whatever is best for John. He's got polit-ical aspirations. Kevin isn't a moron, because you don't get clerkships if you're an idiot, but he doesn't strike me as the type to go above and beyond. If I had to guess, he probably got his clerkship appointment because of his father. He's sloppy and a drunk. He'll probably end up being president one day."

I snorted out a laugh.

"And he's got some control issues because he won't let his girlfriend out of his sight long enough for her to work," I said. "That's a little creepy. But I think it's weird John said Thea was the clingy one. It seems to me like Kevin is possessive and jealous. All three of the girls have had a sexual relationship with John. And jealousy is always a motive for murder."

"True," Jack said. "Or maybe they've played musical beds with more than just John and he's the jealous one. We need more information. All we can do is speculate until we have more."

"Well, if we're moving on to the Hargrove case, you can add this to your other board," I said, handing him the file on Steve Hargrove. "Official ruling is homicide. There's definitely fracturing on the parietal *and* the occipital. A blow like that would have rendered him incapacitated."

"Long enough for someone to put him in the chair and put a shotgun under his chin?" Jack asked.

"Exactly," I said.

"Any idea the kind of weapon for the blunt force we're looking for?"

"It was too small of a sample," I said. "I can

only give an estimate of the actual wound site because I don't have all the pieces of the skull, but I can tell you he wasn't struck with a sharp object. There was no penetration or chipped skull fragments. At least not in the parts of the skull that were recovered."

"Crimes like these are rarely premeditated," Jack said. "Archie Hill showed up on a whim once. He might have done it again. Tempers are high and he just grabs something close by and hits him in the back of the head."

"Only Hill said he was at school during the time of the murder," I said.

"We'll confirm his alibi in the morning. We've got a whole laundry list of people to talk to. If Hargrove really was rebooting his coaching staff and players then there's the potential for a lot of pissed-off people."

"Don't forget parents," I said. "Not to mention administrators, students, and just about anyone who has an interest in general. Football brings in a lot of money for this area. Especially when they're winning. You heard Hill. They've got scouts at every game and practice for that quarterback."

"We need to go back to the scene and look at it from the killer's perspective," Jack said. "Maybe we'll see something new."

There was a knock at the door and Cole stuck his head in. "Got a minute?"

Cole was a modern-day cowboy. His family had owned one of the tobacco farms in Bloody Mary, but they'd had to sell it off when hard times hit. Cole didn't hold any resentment when Jack bought up the property as he'd not liked being a farmer anyway. He wore his usual uniform of Wranglers and an untucked denim shirt with the sheriff's logo on the breast pocket, and his Stetson was already on his head.

He was a handsome man around forty who'd spent his life playing the field. He'd never been married and didn't have any kids, at least that we knew of, and the relationship he had with Lily was the longest he'd ever had. I'd known Cole for a long time. He'd been a cop long before Jack had been elected sheriff. He was a good detective— slow and methodical—and he had a mind for puzzles. I'd always called him Cole. I had no idea what his first name was.

"I've got several minutes," Jack said. "We're not making any headway here."

"Made an arrest on our gasoline guy," Cole said. "Just finished up the paperwork."

"What's the story there?" Jack asked.

"Our vic was newly divorced," Cole said. "Been married twenty-two years and trades in the wife for a younger model. They've got three kids. Youngest is eleven, oldest is twenty-two. And from what I can gather the new girlfriend has some money, so the victim starts telling the wife he's hired the best attorneys and he's going to take the kids and sell the house and leave her with nothing."

"Sounds like a real man," Jack said.

"Yeah, well, I guess something in the wife just snapped," Cole said. "She's known his habits for twenty-two years. And every morning he stops at the gas station on Windsor and Queen Margaret to buy a black coffee, a Red Bull, and a scratch-off. And every morning he parks blocking the alley, puts his drinks on the hood, and then he scratches off his ticket. The wife was waiting for him in the alley when he came out. She'd just filled up a paint bucket of gas. We've got her on security cams. She yells out his name and when he looks up she tosses the gasoline on him. And while he's freaking out and screaming she calmly lights a match and he goes up like a torch."

"Wow," I said. "Just when you think you've heard it all."

Cole grunted in agreement. "I guess there's consequences for being an asshole. The wife gets in her car as calm as you please and drives away.

And the store manager runs out with the fire extinguisher, just hoping the whole place doesn't go up in flames. The victim had third degree burns on more than seventy percent of his body. He only lived about an hour after he got to the hospital."

"That's a terrible way to die," I said, wincing.

"After I'd watched the surveillance tapes I got an arrest warrant for the wife," Cole said. "When I got there she was waiting for me. She'd already made arrangements for the oldest sister to be the permanent guardian of the two younger siblings. And the kids are the beneficiaries in the ex-husband's will and for his life insurance, so she knew they'd be taken care of financially."

"So it's premeditated," Jack said. "She'll go away forever."

"She'll go away somewhere forever," Cole said. "She's crazy as a loon."

"Good work," Jack told him. "At least that's one put away."

"Heard you caught a couple of good ones today," Cole said. "I'm freed up if you need me."

"I need you," Jack said. "The Cami Downey case is going to take some legwork. Found her body in Gambo Creek. But we don't have a murder site or weapon. All we have is a bunch of unlikeable roommates and speculation. And a knife missing from the block in the kitchen."

"You got it, boss," Cole said. "I'm heading out for the night. I need my bed in the worst way."

"Tell Lily thanks again for the work she did on Steve Hargrove," I told him. "She's the one who found the skull fracturing."

He made a face and said, "You'll probably have to tell her yourself. Lily isn't exactly talking to me right now."

"Since when?" I asked. "I thought y'all were good. What happened?"

I looked at Jack. Cole had a reputation for a reason, and we'd both worried about what the fallout of this relationship might be from the beginning. It also made it hard because they weren't just employees, but friends as well.

In all honesty, none of those questions were any of my business and I wouldn't have blamed Cole at all for shutting me down, but I was too surprised to think of a more supportive and neutral response.

"I thought we were good too," he said shrugging. He was acting like he wasn't bothered by the whole thing, but he didn't hide it that well. "We were fine this morning. She's been staying at my place anyway, and we'd already decided she'd give up her apartment next month when her lease ends. And then today I asked her to marry me, and she said no. So I guess that's that."

Jack and I were both standing there with our mouths hanging open. That was not what I'd expected him to say at all.

"You asked Lily to marry you?" Jack asked.

"Yeah," he said. "Bought a ring and everything."

"And she said no?" I asked. "Did she say why?"

"Nope," he said. "Just said she had to get back to work."

"It was a pretty rough day," I said, feeling like I was walking through a minefield. "Sometimes the job hits you when you least expect it and you take it out on the people you love."

"I don't know," he said. "But Lily will do what she wants. We're both adults. I've just reached a point in my life that I realized I don't want my future to look like what my past has been. I want a wife and kids. I just realized I've been waiting all this time for the right person."

"Maybe you should tell Lily that," I said.

Cole grunted and said, "Catch y'all tomorrow."

"Cole," Jack called out, making the other man pause before he closed the door behind him. "My money is on you."

Cole nodded and left.

"What is happening?" I asked after a few moments of silence. "It's like the whole world has gone crazy."

"My brain still hasn't caught up to that conversation," Jack said. "Which means we need to get some sleep and maybe everything we dealt with today will suddenly become clear. Or maybe when we wake up the murderers will decide to do the right thing and make a full confession."

"How come that never happens?" I asked.

"Because people suck," Jack said.

There was a small room at the back of Jack's office, no bigger than a large closet, and it had a full-size bed and a rack with extra clothes and uniform shirts. There was a small bathroom off to the side that had a shower, toilet, and sink. It was efficient and utilitarian, and for tonight, it was home.

Jack locked the door and took off his shirt, tossing it in a corner, and then he stripped out of the rest of his clothes. He flipped off the light and then fell face-first on the bed.

I washed my face and stripped out of my clothes, calculating in my head that if I was lucky I'd get five solid hours of sleep before I had to be back up.

"So," Jack said as I made my way toward the bed. "You want to do it?"

I snorted out a laugh and said, "Yeah, I kind of do."

"Okay, but you've got to do all the work."

And then I pounced on top of him.

CHAPTER NINE

JACK MOVED A LOT FASTER THAN I DID IN THE mornings. He's what some people like to call a morning person. When his eyes opened, he was fully alert and usually had something to say. I had no idea why he'd have so many things to talk about after being asleep.

I was the exact opposite of Jack. I didn't wake up fast and I didn't wake up alert or with enough brain function to form words. So I wasn't surprised when Jack slipped out of bed early and went to shower, leaving me asleep. And I wasn't surprised to wake up with a coffee sitting on the little table next to the bed. What I was surprised to see was the Lady Jane's label across the front.

"I figured you deserved something a little special after doing all the work last night," he said. "There's an apple fritter and a bear claw in the bag."

My eyes hadn't yet focused to see the donut bag, but I could smell the sugar and half crawled my way to a sitting position.

"Emmy Lu will know," I croaked, taking the coffee cup and inhaling the sweet aroma of hazelnut and cream. "And I don't even care. I'm a bad friend."

"It's Saturday," Jack said. "She doesn't work on Saturdays. She'll never know."

I grunted, but I knew the truth. Lady Jane's put a smile on my face that not even sex could replicate.

"Whatimsit?" I slurred.

"Early still," Jack said. "Not yet six. You've got some time to linger. I've got teams coming in this morning so we can start canvassing the areas around Gambo Creek at first light. How long do you think it'll take you to do the autopsy on Danforth?"

"A couple of hours," I said, stifling a yawn.

Jack looked at his phone. "Okay, I'll pick you up at ten and we'll head back over to the Hargroves'."

I gave him a half-hearted thumbs-up and opened the pastry bag. By the time I finished the bear claw I was ready to crawl out of bed and into the shower, so I took my coffee with me and stood under the spray, grateful that I could stand there as long as I wanted and not run out of hot water. I figured with the kind of taxes we paid in Virginia the city could afford a few extra bucks on their water bill.

I was thoroughly satisfied and awake by the time I finished my shower, and I dried off quickly and pulled on the clothes I'd shoved in my bag— black leggings and a soft sweater in the same gray as my eyes. All I had was my rain boots, so I put them on, ran fingers through my hair, and put on ChapStick.

It was just after seven by the time I grabbed my things and made my way out of the sheriff's office.

I blinked my eyes several times and looked up at the sky. There was a sliver of orange sun rising through the clouds. And it wasn't raining.

"Good Lord," I said. "It's the sun."

"Tell me about it," Riley said, passing me on the stairs. He'd already been to Lady Jane's. He was holding two boxes of donuts and a coffee. "I'm going to have to find my sunglasses. It's been so long since I've worn them I can't remember where I put them."

I grunted and said, "Be safe out there." And

then I waved goodbye and made my way across the street to where I'd left the Suburban.

The Towne Square was quiet and empty. The cars from the night before were gone, and all of the bars were closed. Most of the other businesses didn't open until ten. The sunrise was almost symbolic—we'd made it through the night and into a new day.

The Suburban was where I'd left it, and I wondered if the uniforms had ever caught the streaker from the night before.

Since the streets were bare it took less than two minutes for me to get back to the funeral home and get parked under the carport. It took another two minutes for me to get my bag and get the side door unlocked.

I hung my jacket and bag up, and was humming under my breath as I made my way into the kitchen. And I almost had a heart attack when Sheldon popped up from behind the other side of the island.

"Sheldon," I said, grabbing my chest in surprise. "You scared the life out of me."

"It's very rare for people to actually die of fright," he said, blinking at me owlishly behind his thick glasses. "Do you have a preexisting heart condition?"

"Not yet," I said. "I didn't see your car out

front."

"Mother dropped me off on her way to bingo," he said. "I was going to take the other Suburban to the cemetery. The Lichner funeral is this morning at ten."

"At least the rain has stopped and the sun is out," I told him. "Looks like Mrs. Lichner is going to get the graveside service of her dreams after all."

"I was looking for the extra boxes of cookies," he said. "The Wallings had their viewing last night. I've never seen so many giant men. They all looked like lumberjacks and ate everything we had set out except for the napkins."

"People love those cookies." I took a water from the fridge, still floating on the cloud of Lady Jane's coffee and donuts.

"Did you know Americans consume more than three billion cookies per year?" he asked.

"I did not," I said. "But it's nice to know we're doing our best to contribute here at Graves Funeral Home."

Sheldon blinked at me again and said, "I didn't find the boxes."

I sighed, wondering if I was destined to have awkward conversations with Sheldon for eternity. "Emmy Lu moved them to the storage room off her office."

There was another awkward pause and then he said, "Okay," before turning on his heel and leaving me alone in the kitchen.

I looked at the clock and then hurried downstairs. Rooney Danforth was waiting for me, and though his autopsy should be fairly typical, I'd learned from experience it was always good to leave room for a surprise or two.

I finished just before ten o'clock, determining that Rooney Danforth had indeed been overdosed with his erectile dysfunction medication. This had caused his heart to become enlarged, and added to the plaque buildup that had already been hardening his arteries, his heart just couldn't take the added strain.

I sent all my findings to Martinez and wished him luck. A case like this might bring a murder charge, but a good attorney would be able to convince a jury it had been accidental.

I washed and tidied everything up, and then I went back upstairs to see if Jack had arrived. He was sitting at the island, working on his phone.

"You could have come down," I said.

"No I couldn't," he said. "I've already had a cup of coffee and Sheldon gave me cookies."

I smirked. The truth was that Jack hated the smell down in the lab. He could look at horrific crime scenes and not bat an eye at putrefied flesh, but embalming fluid was a smell that lingered and he always turned an interesting shade of green whenever he came downstairs.

"I also learned that Americans eat way too many cookies every year," he said. "No wonder we have an obesity problem."

"Cookies seem like the least of our troubles," I said. "I'm ready to leave when you are. Sheldon is overseeing the funeral this morning."

Jack smiled and slid off the barstool. "He's a useful fellow. And he's stopped throwing up at crime scenes. He'll be entering manhood before we know it."

I laughed and grabbed my jacket and bag, and then my laughter faded as I looked out the kitchen window.

"What happened to the sun?" I asked glumly, watching the rain splatting against the windows.

"Just a figment of your imagination," he said. "Cheer up. It's only supposed to last a few more days."

"We'll all be underwater by then," I said. "We'll be like the new Atlantis, just dropped off into the Potomac and covered with water. Two thousand years from now they'll find that giant statue of the beaver that's in front of the university and all of our cell phones and think we were a primitive society that worshipped large rodents."

"How many cups of coffee have you had this morning?" Jack asked.

"Just the one."

"Maybe you need another," he said, and we made a quick break for Jack's truck.

"How are the roads?" I asked once we were on the way.

"Better," he said. "We should be able to go home tonight. The tree crews have been out. We had several fallen trees that were blocking the flow of water so the creeks couldn't drain out. Power line crews have been out all night too. There's not too much damage. A few homes flooded that are on the creek line, but they're in the flood plain so it's nothing new. One of the school busses got stuck in the mud yesterday, so it's still blocking part of the road. But the kids got transported out safely. Everyone else is just wet and grumpy."

"Is Mrs. Hargrove staying with the neighbors?" I asked.

"Not sure," Jack said. "We can go over and find out. I didn't want to tell her over the phone that her husband was murdered."

The Hargrove house looked sad and vacant when we pulled into the driveway. The police units were gone, and Steve Hargrove's truck sat alone in the driveway. The crime scene tape stretched across the porch, and there was a package that the mailman left sitting half under the porch, so the end of it was damp from the rain.

Jack pulled the crime scene tape back so I could duck under, and then he picked up the damp package and put it under his arm. The front door was unlocked and we stepped inside the now-familiar house.

There was still the lingering smell of death in the air, but now there was a staleness along with it. The front entry floors were grimy with so many people traipsing in and out of the house the day before.

I handed Jack a pair of gloves and then put the strap of my bag across my chest so I could move more freely. I put my own gloves on and tried to look at the house in a different light now that I knew for sure we were dealing with a homicide.

"Anything on the doorbell camera during the time of the murder?" I asked.

"Well," Jack said. "Interestingly enough, the app shows that the camera went offline on Thursday afternoon and never came back on."

"On purpose?" I asked.

"I don't think so," he said. "The entire neighborhood went offline. Most of them automatically came back online within a couple of hours. But it probably had to be done manually and if the Hargroves didn't realize it wasn't working they wouldn't have known they needed to get reconnected."

"So the killer could have come in the front or back door," I said. "Neighbors are far enough apart to where they'd have to be looking specifically at the right time and place to see anyone pull up to the house. Time of death was prime time for neighbors that might have been leaving for work."

"Martinez is going to follow up with the ones who weren't home yesterday," Jack said. "No signs of forced entry. The tech guys pulled lots of fingerprints inside the house and on the doors as well. Mrs. Hargrove said neighbors pop in and out often, not to mention she's got a daughter and son-in-law and grandkids that are local and visit frequently."

"Same kind of traffic in the office?" I asked.

"Pretty much," Jack said. "Hargrove liked to show off his trophies and memorabilia. When they had cookouts or staff parties he'd always bring people in his office to show them around."

Coach Hargrove's office had been thoroughly

searched by the forensic team. There was a light coating of powder from the techs over every surface that might have fingerprints. The victim and brain matter and tissues had all been removed, but the walls and floors were badly stained. The crime scene cleanup team would have a job to do once this was all over.

"He's getting ready to leave for the morning," Jack said. "His stuff is sitting in the entryway. And someone shows up at the door."

"Or someone makes themselves at home and comes inside," I said, remembering what Lydia had said about neighbors popping in and out all the time and the doors being unlocked.

"Whoever it was, Hargrove brought him back to the office," Jack said. "If it was me I'd be trying to rush them along and get them out the door so I could leave for work."

"Unless it's someone you know well," I said. "Someone who said it was important they talked to you. Hargrove would make the time then."

"Yeah," Jack sighed. "You're right. This is personal. It's emotional. Whoever the killer is didn't come over with the intention to kill. They didn't bring their own weapon. They used what was on hand. Tempers flared and anger got the best of them."

Jack took my arms and moved me. He stood

right in front of the desk and he positioned me in front of him. And then I looked around for the closest thing to grab.

"The helmet," I said, pointing to the shelves where several red helmets sat. It was his trophy wall, that archived every state championship he'd won over the last thirty years. There were seven floating shelves that held red helmets with the year stickered on the side, along with the team pictures and the trophies. But one of the helmets was missing. I'd noticed it the day before, but I hadn't been thinking of it in terms of a murder weapon.

"Something like that would cause the fracturing on the skull. It's rounded so the impact point is spread out across the surface instead of leaving a sharp impact point, and it would also explain the red flakes we found. It was paint."

"And Coach Hargrove wouldn't think twice about turning his back," Jack said.

"Because he trusted whoever it was," I said, nodding.

I reached up to the shelf and said, "It's a little tall for me to reach. I'd have to stand on my toes to reach the shelf. The killer would lose the element of surprise if it wasn't a quick and smooth motion to crack the helmet in the back of his skull."

"So we're looking for someone taller than you," Jack said, lips twitching. "That narrows it down."

"Shut up," I said, smiling. I reached up and took one of the other helmets from the shelf, feeling its weight and then passing it over to Jack. "So your back is turned to me and I slam the helmet into your skull, immediately rendering you unconscious. And then you fall forward. Maybe across the desk? Or maybe straight to the floor."

"Coach wasn't a big guy," Jack said. "What was he? Five ten or eleven?"

"Ten," I said. "Seventy-nine point three kilograms. He was in good shape. Lots of muscle so that put him on the heavier side."

"What is that in American?" Jack asked.

"A hundred and seventy-five pounds," I said. "Of dead weight."

"That's not easy to do from any position," Jack said. "Much less if the killer had to pick him up from the floor."

"Where was the gun?" I asked. "If I'm the killer and I just knock a guy unconscious I'd probably be freaking out a little if it was the result of pure emotion. I'd be scrambling, trying to figure out what to do. You've only got two choices at that point. You can do the right thing and call in the EMTs and wait with him until he regains consciousness. Or you can finish him off. This person decides to finish him off."

"So they have to figure out how they're going to do it," Jack said, taking up my train of thought. "The sawed-off shotgun is the easy choice. If you know that Coach has one and where it is."

"Yeah," I said, getting a sinking feeling in my stomach. "We need to go talk to Joe Able. One thing that's not explained is how he avoided the blowback of blood spatter and brain matter. We'd have noticed the inconsistency in pattern if he'd been standing over the body to pull the trigger."

"Yeah, that takes a cooler head," Jack said. "You have to know how weapons work and the best way to avoid being covered in evidence." Jack moved behind the desk where Coach Hargrove had been sitting in the leather chair. "I get him lifted and settled in the chair. Go get the gun. Time is of the essence I'm guessing. How long would someone stay unconscious with a head injury like that?"

"It could be anywhere from fifteen minutes to hours," I said. "It would depend on the damage done to the brain, which I wasn't able to observe in the autopsy since his brain was gone."

"The killer might be thinking they don't have

a lot of time," Jack said. "So they're moving fast. Go get the gun and then take the time to position him. There were powder burns on Hargrove's right hand, so he was definitely holding the weapon when it was fired."

"So how do you do it?" I asked.

"Easy," he said and crawled under the space beneath the desk.

It was a tight fit for someone Jack's size. "Joe Able is about your size."

"Yeah," Jack said. "It's definitely a tight squeeze. It's hard to maneuver, but doable." He reached out and grabbed the leather chair, pulling it toward him. "Joe Able is in good shape. He's a big guy. He could easily lift Hargrove and put him in the chair and then pull it to him from down here. But no one's prints are on the weapon but Hargrove's."

"So he positions the gun, pulls the trigger and kills him," I said. "And then wipes his prints from the weapon?"

Jack grunted and looked at his own gloved hands. "I want to bring the fingerprint techs back out and have them look for prints on the underside of the chair and down here under the desk. Let's pay a visit next door and talk to Joe Able."

CHAPTER TEN

IT WAS A SOMBER WALK TO THE ABLES' HOUSE NEXT door. It was even worse knowing Mrs. Hargrove was probably staying with the man who killed her husband. Sometimes the people we were closest to, who we loved, were just disappointing.

The Able house was a red-brick Colonial with a circular drive in front. There was a three-car garage, and Lydia's little red RAV4 was parked in front of one of the bays.

The rain wasn't as heavy as it had been the day before—just a soaking mist—but the temperature was cooling and I found myself wishing I had warmer clothes to wear.

"I really don't want to do this," I said, as we stood in front of the door. "She's already been through so much."

"We're just here to talk to him," Jack said, ringing the doorbell. "That's all we can do until we can get some proof."

"Sheriff," Ada Able said when she opened the door. "Dr. Graves. Come in, come in. Get out of the wet. Lydia is here if you're looking for her."

"We'd like to talk to her for a few minutes if she's able," Jack said. "We won't take up much of her time."

Ada was dressed in yoga pants and an oversized T-shirt, and she was wearing sneakers.

"Sorry, you caught me in the middle of my workout," she said. "I haven't really known what to do with myself this morning. Lydia wanted some alone time to start making arrangements and Derek and Joe went up to the school with the rest of the team. The principal called an impromptu memorial service. This has been so hard on the kids."

I guessed we wouldn't be talking to Joe Able after all.

"Let me run and get Lydia for you," she said. "You can make yourselves comfortable in the front living room."

"We'll go by the school," Jack said, reading my mind. "I don't want to let too much time pass." He was on his phone, rapidly sending a text. "I want the fingerprint techs back here now.

Able has open access to the house. I don't want him going back over in case there's evidence we missed."

"It would help if he had the helmet in his trunk or something," I said.

"We'll get there," Jack said. "All we have right now is suspicion. I don't have enough to get a search warrant for anyone."

I heard the footsteps coming down the hall and Lydia peeked around the doorframe. "Jack... Jaye," she said. "I didn't think I'd see you back so soon. Is it... Are you finished with everything? When can I have Steve back?" Then she looked at me and my heart broke at the brave face she was trying to put on. But the grief in her eyes was plain for anyone to see.

"Come in and sit down," Jack said, taking her gently by the arm. "We'll talk about all of that. Do you want something to drink?"

I was surprised at the chuckle she gave as she shook her head. "I may never drink anything again. I've been plied with enough tea and warm whiskey to float a battleship."

I knew the best way to handle Mrs. Hargrove was with facts and being straightforward. She wasn't a wilting flower. She'd taught first graders for decades. That took a special amount of fortitude.

"I should have all the paperwork finished this afternoon," I said.

She nodded briskly. "I talked with my daughter last night and we decided it was probably best to have him cremated. We'll do a big memorial service at the church and put his picture up. That's how people should remember him."

"That will be a lovely tribute," I told her. "You know I had to do an autopsy on him. It's standard procedure."

"Yes," she said. "I know. Another reason for deciding on the cremation."

"During the autopsy my assistant discovered fracturing along the back of Coach's skull," I told her.

Her brow furrowed in confusion. "What does that mean?"

"It means that he didn't take his life," I said. "Someone struck him on the back of the head. And then they made it look like he killed himself."

Lydia froze—even her breathing stopped for a few seconds. And then she exhaled loudly and pressed her fingers to her eyes.

"I knew it," she said. "I knew he wouldn't. I knew he'd never do such a thing. It didn't make sense. We had such a nice morning together. We have such a nice life. A fulfilling life. We don't have financial problems, our daughter is happily married with her own family. We've been talking about what we want to do for the rest of our lives. We're not so old yet that we can't still have fun. Maybe travel."

"Was Coach planning on retiring?" Jack asked.

She sighed and shook her head. "That was our one point of contention. He was supposed to retire this year. I wanted him to. I was thinking how wonderful it would be not to have to go through another training camp and football season. I've been a coach's wife for a lot of years. When our daughter was home it was like being a single mother. If we wanted to see him we'd pack up and go to practices and every football game."

"He changed his mind?" Jack asked.

She nodded slowly. "He was a good man. A man of integrity. And he said he'd be doing a disservice to the students and everyone in this community if he didn't build the team back up before he left. He thought it would take him another two to three years."

"I thought he had a good team," Jack said. "What was going on?"

She sighed and looked toward the door. "It's not easy to talk about. And it's really put a strain on our friendship with the Ables since their son is part of it. Steve has had a talented group of players the past couple of years. But there's something about this generation...lots of attitude and entitlement. They think they can skip practices or their teachers will pass them just because they play football. Steve sat all his starters for a game last fall because they all skipped out on an evening practice to go to some party. Parents and his coaches gave him hell, but he didn't care and the principal backed him up. Steve has always said he cares more about raising up good men then winners.

"And several of them have grade issues too. I know for a fact Derek and Eli are both failing and will probably have to do summer school and make up credits next fall. Which means they won't get to play football unless they could convince Steve to keep them on the team. And you can imagine the snowball effect that's having. Both of those boys have been scouted since their freshman year and have already had offers to commit to Dı colleges. But Steve wasn't going to play them. He has a strict no-pass, no-play rule."

"So that's why he needs to rebuild the team," Jack said, understanding. "That's a hard spot to be in. There aren't a lot of men who would hold the line with that kind of integrity."

Her smile trembled. "Well, there weren't a lot of men like Steve. He'd already talked to the school board and the superintendent. Steve told them it was time to wipe the slate clean, and it was a privilege to be part of a winning organization like ours. He's had problems with this batch the last couple of years. Archie Hill undermining him at every turn, causing division and disloyalty among the coaches, and playing favorites to the kids Steve keeps having to discipline. Those kids are more disrespectful every time they walk into class. It was just a bad situation all around.

"So Steve told them he wants to hire a whole new coaching staff next year, and he's going to cut any player who isn't academically meeting the marks, but also any player who needs an attitude adjustment in general. There's a good crop of freshman coming up, and he said he could build a team out of anyone who worked hard and really wanted to be there."

"And Derek Able is one of those kids?" Jack asked. "That must have been very hard."

"You have no idea," she said. "Joe and Lydia haven't spoken to us for the last couple of weeks. But we've been friends a long time, so I was glad to see them yesterday."

"Did Steve and Joe have a confrontation?" Jack asked.

"Boy, did they," Lydia said. "Right in the backyard. It was right after Steve had met with his administration and told them what he wanted to do. Those meetings are closed door and supposed to be private, but someone spilled the beans, and it wasn't long before we were getting phone calls from the newspaper and meeting requests with angry parents. Steve sent an email out to all his players and the parents talking about rumors and distractions and that when there was information to give they'd hear directly from him about it. That calmed most of them down, but Joe came over while Steve was barbecuing out back one evening. It was a Sunday so our daughter and her family were here, and we'd invited Don and Lynnell Wilkes from down the street. They'd had to put their dog down and it seemed like they needed the company."

"What did Joe want?" Jack asked, trying to get her to focus back on the question.

She checked the door again to make sure we were alone. "He came over all smiles at first. Like usual. But then he started talking about what he'd heard from one of the administrators at school. Joe is a broker, and I guess he's been doing some investing for some of the higher paid employees of the district without taking a fee, so they felt comfortable coming to him when they saw things were about to be shaken up.

"Joe asked Steve point-blank if the rumors were true, and Steve being Steve told him that changes had to be made for the greater good. That's when Joe started yelling about how Steve wasn't going to screw up Derek's chances of getting into the school of his choice, and then Steve yelled back that if Derek couldn't pass eleventh grade, why would he want him to go off and fail college. Derek is a smart kid, mind you, and Joe and Ada are both well educated. But Derek expects things handed to him on a silver platter. He has a terrible work ethic and he's not the most respectful kid. Joe and Ada both laugh it off as teenage years and hormones, but it's more than that. They bought him a brand-new Jeep when he got his license and he wrecked it the first week he had it. He'd been drinking and went into a ditch."

"I didn't hear about that," Jack said. "No report was filed."

"That's because Joe took care of it. There wasn't damage to anything but the Jeep, and it was on his own property where the accident happened. The cops weren't called, the Jeep got towed, and Derek got a free pass. They bought him a Hummer a few weeks later. I guess that was their way of trying to keep him safe."

"Sounds like they're not doing him any favors," I said.

"No," she said, shaking her head. "I love Joe and Lydia like family, but they've done that boy a great disservice. And Eli is a follower. He'll do anything that Derek is doing."

"Did the argument get physical?" I asked.

"I thought it would," she said. "We all heard the yelling so we were watching at the back window. But all of a sudden Joe seemed to get control of himself and he walked back over to his house. That was two weeks ago, and he didn't approach Steve again. Not even when the school board had their meeting Wednesday night for contract renewals and Steve's entire coaching staff wasn't renewed."

"Tell us about the shotgun," Jack said. "Where did he usually keep it?"

Her lips pressed tight together at the mention of the gun and her fingers clamped together. "The top shelf of my kitchen pantry," she said. "He wanted to keep it out of the way of the grandkids, but he wanted it handy. One of Steve's few hobbies was feeding the birds and cataloguing the different ones that came to visit in the backyard. I always made fun of him and asked if he could have picked any more of an old man hobby."

She chuckled to herself, lost in a memory we would never know. "But when Steve put the food out the squirrels saw that as an open invitation. He had all kinds of contraptions out there. He'd greased the poles and bought some machine off the internet that would fling the squirrels across the yard. But every time he tried something new they'd eventually figure out how to get past it. So that's when he started using the shotgun. Thank God we live in a neighborhood where everyone has some land and space between their houses. The only neighbors who can really hear the gunshots are Ada and Joe."

"How many people knew where Steve kept the gun?"

"Oh, gosh," she said. "Everyone knew. It was rare for any company to come over where Steve didn't talk about those stupid squirrels and then show everyone how he dealt with them."

"Thank you, Mrs. Hargrove," Jack said. "We won't take up any more of your time."

"Time is all I've got," she said, getting to her feet and walking us to the door. "I'm not sure what to do next. I want to be in my home, but at the same time I don't want to be there. But I know I can't stay here too much longer."

"We've done almost everything we can do over there," Jack said. "I'm thinking I can have a cleaning crew come over tomorrow and put everything back to rights for you. And then you can do whatever is best for you."

Jack's hand was on the doorknob when Mrs. Hargrove put her hand on Jack's shoulder. "I want to thank both of you." Her eyes misted with tears and I had to blink back my own. "I know what the easy choice would have been after walking in on the scene you did yesterday. And I know you fought for him. None of this is easy, but knowing you fought for him helps. I just wanted to tell you that."

I'm not the most affectionate person, but I pulled her into a hug and held her fragile body close to mine. Holding back tears wasn't going to happen, and I felt them drip slowly down my cheeks.

It was easy to lose sight of the mission when you were mired in the muck day after day. But this was the reason we did what we did. It was because people like Coach Hargrove didn't have anyone to speak for them, and they deserved better.

CHAPTER ELEVEN

"Well," Jack said, once we were back in the car. His voice was hoarse, and I could tell he'd been just as moved as I had.

"Yeah," I said, feeling a resolve deep inside of me that I hadn't felt for a long time. "Let's go find a killer."

"Let's see if anyone is still at the high school," he said. "Maybe we can catch multiple birds with one stone."

There had been one high school in King George County for decades, and it was in Bloody Mary since Bloody Mary had the most land for the football stadium and sports complex. But the county was increasing at such a rapid pace that one high school wasn't going to work for too much longer. The school had tried to pass a bond for a second high school the year before and there'd been so much opposition and arguments that they'd decided to wait another couple of years before they put it on the ballot again.

That was the thing about living in a place like King George County. The people here were strong in tradition and family values, and people took pride in the same surnames passing from generation to generation and staying close to home. They also hated change. I'd been in high school when the public library got the internet for the first time, and there'd almost been a brawl in the Towne Square.

The parking lot of King George High School was half full of cars. There were students and parents in the lot, lingering over conversation before getting back in the vehicles and driving away.

"Let's try the field house," Jack said. "There are still a lot of cars parked there."

Jack parked his truck and turned his lights on, and I climbed out, dread lodging in the pit of my stomach. After talking to Mrs. Hargrove, I realized this was a very volatile situation. Joe Able had the means, motive, and opportunity. But as angry as the parents and students were, anyone else could have killed Coach Hargrove under the right circumstances.

His morning routine was as consistent as the sunrise, and so was Mrs. Hargrove's for that matter. She went to the grocery store every Friday morning. It wasn't a secret that Coach had a shotgun, what he used it for, and where he kept it. Maybe it was premeditated. Maybe someone had two weeks to work up a full head of steam and went over there with the intent to kill and cover it up as a suicide. People often thought they could commit the perfect murder. They were almost always wrong.

"Sheriff," Mary Cormac said as we made our way along the sidewalk to the field house.

I knew Mary was the school board president. She'd been on the board when Jack and I had been in school. She was a forbidding figure, even though her stature was only a couple of inches over five feet. Her posture was ramrod straight and her steel-gray hair was curled and teased on top and cut short with military precision. Frown lines and crow's feet were etched on her face, and her eyes were puffy and red rimmed from crying.

Standing next to her was Corbin Maxwell, whose bald, egg-shaped head I'd recognize anywhere. He'd been the algebra teacher when I was in school, but I'd heard he was an administrator now. And next to him was an attractive

African American woman who looked to be in her mid-forties.

"Mary," Jack said, reaching out to shake her hand. "How are you?"

"I've been better," she said, shaking her head. "A terrible thing about Coach Hargrove. And poor Lydia. I don't know how she's dealing with this. Just terrible."

"I never would have thought Steve would be the type to kill himself," Corbin said, his mustache quivering in agitation.

"That's why we're here," Jack said. "Steve Hargrove didn't kill himself. He was murdered."

There were three gasps of surprise followed by stunned silence.

"Who would do such a thing?" Mary finally muttered, looking back and forth between her colleagues.

"Who wouldn't do such a thing with everything going on around here lately," the woman I didn't know said.

"Sheriff Jack Lawson," Jack said, reaching out a hand to the woman. "I didn't catch your name."

"Oh, I'm sorry, Sheriff," Mary said, pressing her fingers to her lips in distraction. It was obvious she was upset by the latest news. "I should have introduced you. I always just assume that everyone knows Alex."

"Alexandra Dixon," she said, returning Jack's handshake. "I'm the principal here at the high school."

"She's Danny's daughter," Corbin said.

Alex smiled. "Years of grad school and getting my PhD, and all I'm known for around here is being Danny's daughter."

Jack and I both grinned in response. We knew exactly how she felt. That was part of the legacy of living in a place like this. If people didn't know your mama or your daddy, then they probably didn't think you were worth knowing at all. Lineage mattered.

"You'll never get away from it," Jack said. "I still have to explain to people that I'm Rich Lawson's son and am not some city interloper trying to corrupt the county."

I figured this was a conversation I'd let Jack and Alex have. I never wanted to bring up my own parents in conversation.

"We just finished speaking with Mrs. Hargrove," Jack said. "She filled us in on the shake-up here at the school. She said there are a lot of people who are upset."

"Upset is an understatement," Alex said, wincing. "But we all knew it would be when Steve came to us. But he was right to do what he did. He cares..." She stopped and swallowed. "He *cared* more about those kids than any teacher I've ever met. Winning games and football is a secondary purpose, he always said. He said his job was to make good men, husbands, and fathers. He was a great man."

"Can you walk us through how this started?" Jack asked. "When did Steve decide change was in order?"

Mary sighed and said, "I guess it was with me. My husband and I have been friends with Steve and Lydia for a lot of years. We'd go over there for dinner sometimes and we'd talk and reminisce. Steve was going to retire at the end of this year. He'd run his plan by me when he wanted to hire Archie Hill as his assistant. Steve is the one who interviews and hires all his coaches, but the school board has to approve them all." She stopped and shook her head. "I told Steve I thought Archie was going to be a problem. He was used to being the head coach, and being in charge isn't an easy thing to stop doing. But Steve had a lot of compassion for the guy. Archie was up front about what happened at his last job and he wanted his marriage and family to succeed. Steve believes in second chances, and Archie knows his stuff, so we hired him.

"But Archie was poison to those boys right

from the start," Mary said. "Archie was the fun coach. The one who would let things slide. Those boys thought a little bit of God-given talent was enough and that the extra practices and requirements weren't necessary for them. Things got pretty hostile in the locker room over the last couple of years."

"Same with the coaching staff," Corbin interjected. "A couple of those guys were loyal to Steve, but they learned real fast that Archie and his boys' club could make life miserable for them if they didn't do things the way he wanted them done."

"Miserable how?" Jack asked.

"Petty stuff," Corbin said. "The offensive line coach would mix up plays for the offensive coordinator. Lots of miscommunication. The kids would be privy to the new plays, but it would leave Steve's guys looking like they didn't know what they were doing. Other things like changing times for team meetings so the coaches who supported Steve would end up in the wrong location or missing them altogether. Missing playbooks. All kinds of childish things."

"I knew Steve had hired Archie with a plan of succession in mind," Mary said. "But he knew it was a disaster almost from the start. But things got worse this last year when Archie's wife left him. He started drinking a lot, and there were rumors going around he was drinking with the kids. A couple of the guys ended up failing drug tests and they were kicked off the team immediately. It was just a real hornet's nest. But Steve has integrity, and he also understands legacy and reputation. He told me he just couldn't in good conscience go out like this. Because it would have been his name people remembered as letting things go to hell."

"That's when he told you his plan to start fresh?" I asked.

Mary blew out a breath. "Oh, yeah. I couldn't blame him, but I told him to take some time to think about it. Steve was never a dummy. He's a strategist, which is why he was a great coach. So he was careful who he talked to at first. He wanted to get a feel for things. Know who his allies were. It turned out he presented such a solid case for doing the right thing that it was pretty unanimous for the changes to be made."

"Who opposed?" Jack asked.

"Only Clyde Warren on the school board," Mary said.

"I met with Steve and the superintendent together," Alex said. "I wanted them both to know I was in full support of this. Those boys are suffering academically, and that will always be my first priority. Dr. Keegan—he's the superintendent—was hesitant at first. It doesn't take a fool to know the outcome of a move like this. But Keegan has weathered storms before. We tried to keep it close to the vest. But after the school board meeting Clyde Warren was the first to start the fire. He called Archie Hill right away and let him know what happened. And then Archie started calling parents. By the next morning I had a stack of emails and voicemails from angry parents and teachers."

"Don't forget the news," Mary said, rolling her eyes. "It was exactly the spectacle we expected it to be. We renewed Steve's contract for another two years and told him to do what he thought was best with his team. Steve had a lot of skin in the game. It would have been foolish of us not to trust him to do what was best."

"Anyone besides Archie Hill you can think of who'd want to do Steve harm?" Jack asked.

"I hate to say it," Mary said sadly. "But after the last two weeks, I think I'd have a list longer than my arm. We don't live in the same world we did when I started on the school board. These parents...they'll do whatever it takes to make sure their kid gets the best and succeeds, despite the kids not earning it. There's no accountability anymore. And people are willing to cheat and lie to get to the top and pull anyone who's in their way down along the way. I wanted to stand up and cheer for Steve Hargrove during that school board meeting. And I think if Clyde Warren had been armed he'd have shot Steve right there in front of everyone. I've never seen a man so angry. He doesn't even have a kid on the team."

"We're looking for Joe Able," I said. "Have you seen him around?"

"He was at the memorial," Alex said. "He and Derek sat with the rest of the team. We held it in the gymnasium. Last I saw they were walking out toward the field house."

"Now that Steve is gone," Jack said. "Are there plans to continue with what Steve wanted?"

Mary chewed on her bottom lip. "We've not renewed several of the coaches' contracts, including Archie's. But we've got to do the best thing for the kids, and what they need right now is stability and a familiar face. Coach White was loyal to Steve and would want to see his legacy and values continue. I'd prefer to keep him on and move him into the head spot, but we've got to come to a consensus. As far as the team is concerned, grades are going to play themselves out. If some of those guys fail classes or drug tests, they're out. It's that simple. Rules are rules. But we'll see how it all shakes out."

Jack nodded and said, "Thank you all for your time."

"You find who did this, Sheriff," Mary said. "They need to pay."

"We'll find them," Jack assured her.

CHAPTER TWELVE

"It's hard not to draw preconceived conclusions with this one," I said. "The people who love and support Steve *really* love and support him. No one has said a bad word against him. Even Archie Hill's only complaint is that he was outdated in his coaching techniques."

"I know," Jack said, holding the door open for me to the field house. "I know the kind of man Coach was because he's always been this way. But hearing the stories from other people...how could you not be on his side? Which makes it that much harder not to immediately villainize anyone who opposed him. Opposition doesn't make a murderer."

"You should put that on a T-shirt," I said.

I followed Jack into a weight room where a

couple of teenagers were already lifting weights, and then into a larger room that had turf and a line of football sleds. There were a lot of teenagers in this room, along with several adults. Archie Hill stood in the center of them, but I couldn't hear what he was saying. I didn't see Joe Able anywhere.

Archie spotted me and Jack and the huddle of guys broke up, but most lingered close by.

"This isn't a great time, Sheriff," Archie said. "It's been an intense morning."

"For us too," Jack said. "Especially since Coach Hargrove was murdered."

Jack said it loud enough to get a reaction, and the volume of voices amped up. There was no change of expression on Archie's face.

"That doesn't change the fact that he's dead, and these kids need time and space to grieve. It doesn't matter how they felt about him. When you spend that much time with a person it makes a dent in your life when they're gone."

"Sage words," Jack said dryly. "How did they feel about him?"

"He was their coach," Archie said. "He kicked their butts every day of every week. He drove them hard. Not everyone performs well when they're coached like that." Archie shrugged it off.

"I'm looking for Joe Able," Jack said. "Have you seen him around?"

"That's my dad," one of the kids said, moving closer to Archie. "What do you want with him?"

Derek Able was a good-looking kid. He was a solid mix of both his parents—tall, mixed race, dark hair like his mother and the blue eyes of his father. He was built like an athlete. There were some people you could look at and tell that they were something special. This kid had that persona that surrounded him. But the sneer and the belligerent expression on his face made me instantly dislike him. Or maybe I'd just been swayed by Lydia's assessment of him.

"Is he still here?" Jack asked, ignoring the question.

"He left a few minutes ago," Derek said. "He said he had to go into the office."

"Okay," Jack said. "We'll catch him later." And he turned to leave, but Derek stopped him.

"That's it?" Derek asked. "You say someone killed Coach Hargrove and then you ask for my dad, and we're not supposed to wonder why?"

Jack looked at me and shook his head. "Why is everyone giving me attitude lately?"

"Must be all the rain," I said dryly. "It short-circuits people's brain cells."

"What's that supposed to mean?" Derek said, taking a step forward.

Jack arched a brow and said, "Son, you're going to want to get down from whatever high horse you're on, and take a step back."

"Walk it off, Able," Archie said, putting a hand on his shoulder. "We're all grieving in different ways. This is an intense situation for all of us. We're all struggling with how to deal with this."

Jack grunted and looked at Archie. "I guess while I'm here I can get some information. I can start with you," Jack said, pointing at Derek. "What time did you get to school yesterday morning?"

Derek looked like he wanted to argue, but Archie squeezed his shoulder again.

"I always get here right at seven fifteen for an early workout," he said.

"Who else was here?" Jack asked.

Derek narrowed his eyes but answered. "I picked Eli up on the way, so he was here with me. Coach Hill was here getting things set up. Troy over there pulled up about the same time as us. And Grit and Flank showed up about seven thirty. Most of the other guys got here closer to eight, but we have weight training first period so we just stay in here most of the morning. Is that what you want to know?"

"Yeah," Jack said. "That's what I wanted to know. About what time did you leave your house?"

"Around six forty-five," he said. "Picked up Eli right at seven."

"You see anyone out in your neighborhood when you were leaving?"

Derek paused for a few seconds, finally looking like he was taking the questions seriously. He licked his lips. "Just Mrs. Hargrove. She was pulling out of her driveway and didn't see me. I had to swerve around her. She always goes to the grocery store on Fridays."

"Thanks," Jack said, and handed him a business card. "Tell your dad to give me a call as soon as he can. He heard the shot and we wanted to check timing with him again."

Derek nodded, and I didn't know if he'd pass the word on to his father, but someone would. Archie Hill had been looking on in fascination. It was better for them to think we needed confirmation rather than them think he was a suspect. People tended to get jumpy when they were suspects.

When we were back in the car I put my hand on Jack's arm. "I'm going to need some coffee soon and something for sustenance. I think my Lady Jane's has worn off, and I'm about thirteen minutes away from hangry."

"That's a little too close for comfort as far as I'm concerned," he said. "The taco place is the closest. But they have terrible coffee. And no one drinks coffee with tacos anyway."

"I'll switch to sodas," I said. "I need the sugar rush."

"How you're not an obese diabetic blows my mind," Jack said.

"Hey, I eat my vegetables and mostly healthy meals," I said. "I just need little snacks and pick-me-ups to get through the day. Those calories don't count because they get burned up fast since I'm in between meals."

Jack shook his head. "Aren't you supposed to be a doctor?"

"Yep, and that's the theory I'm sticking to. You've got seven minutes to make a taco appear in my hand."

"Good thing I work best under that kind of pressure," he said.

"You work best under all kinds of pressure," I said. "I'll show you later. But tacos first."

He laughed and got in line at the drive-thru.

"It's just after noon. Why does it feel like we've already put in a full day's work?"

"Because we have," I said.

"Let's take all this back to the office," Jack said. "I want to touch base with Cole on Cami Downey, and the roommate crew are supposed to come in at half hour intervals starting at one thirty for interview."

"Your ability to multitask is very sexy," I said. "I suppose I need to check in with Sheldon and make sure no one drowned at the funeral this morning."

"Was that a concern?" Jack asked, taking bags of tacos from the girl at the window.

"He was having dreams about pushing Mrs. Lichner into the coffin with her husband."

Jack winced. "I can see how you might be concerned. You just never know with Sheldon. I wouldn't be surprised to see his picture on a milk carton because he'd been kidnapped, but I also wouldn't be surprised if I saw his picture pop up on *America's Most Wanted*."

"He's versatile, our Sheldon," I said.

Thinking of Sheldon and Mrs. Lichner had me a little worried, so I called him on the way back to the sheriff's office.

"Everything's fine," Sheldon said when he answered the phone.

That was not the typical greeting and I immediately became suspicious. "What happened?" I asked.

He was silent on the other end of the line.

"Sheldon?"

"I figured you'd already gotten a phone call," he said. "Sometimes it's easier to relay the story when you already know what's coming."

"You are not putting me at ease, Sheldon," I said, glancing at Jack. His eyes were on the road but his lips were twitching.

"Well..." Sheldon said.

"Did you push Mrs. Lichner into her husband's grave?"

Sheldon gasped. "Of course not," he said. "But Mrs. Lichner's sister warned me when the family showed up that all of Bruce's brothers had hosted a wake at the house last night. They were all drunk when they showed up this morning."

"What about Mrs. Lichner?" I asked.

"She can sure hold her liquor," he said. "A woman can typically only have four drinks within a two-hour period before she starts to suffer from alcohol poisoning."

"But Mrs. Lichner beat that?"

"She was drinking something that smelled like cherry cough syrup from a flask in her purse all through the ceremony. Her sister said she watched her drink a bottle of wine with her waffles that morning, and that on the way to the funeral in the limo one of Bruce's brothers gave her a shot of moonshine."

"It's a wonder she could stand up straight," I said.

"She couldn't," Sheldon said.

"Sheldon, just tell me what happened." I rubbed at the headache brewing at the base of my neck.

"Well, we'd already installed the burial vault because of the rain, and the casket was sitting on top of the lowering device like usual, so no one could have fallen in Bruce's grave. But we didn't put the burial vault in Merilee Walling's grave yet because we had to get the equipment out because of the rain, and her funeral isn't until tomorrow anyway."

"Yes," I said, plugging my phone into the car so Sheldon's voice came out through the speakers. I reclined my seat back and closed my eyes, inhaling the scent of tacos from the bag.

"So Mrs. Lichner got upset during the service and started crying real loud, and then she got up during the eulogy and pushed the preacher out the way and started saying how she wasn't sure how she was going to be able to go on without Bruce, and how he'd taken care of her for the last forty years. It was very touching."

I hmmed and dug in the bag for a taco. Two minutes was too long to wait until we got to the sheriff's office and I just needed something to tide me over.

"And then she just kind of stumbled off, and everyone just sat there because there wasn't much left to say after that and the preacher was still on the ground where she'd pushed him. Then she wandered over to the area where we'd dug Merilee Walling's grave, but she ignored the barriers we had set up. It was like slow motion. She took a drink from her flask and slipped in the mud, and she kind of slid feetfirst. We had a couple of boards over the hole, but her momentum dislodged one of them and she slid right in."

"You're kidding me," I said. And then I coughed profusely as I swallowed the wrong way. "Sheldon...this is not funny."

"So we called 911," he continued. "But she was already dead by the time they arrived."

"Oh, God," I said, feeling the blood drain from my face.

"But I don't think you'll get sued or anything,"

Sheldon said. "There were a whole lot of witnesses, including a preacher, so everyone will believe his story. And we had all the protections and everything up like protocol demands."

There was an awkward silence and Sheldon said, "Just thought you should know." And then he disconnected.

I started on my second taco.

"You okay?" Jack asked after several minutes of silence. He parked in his spot and turned off the car.

"Yep," I said. "Some things are out of our control. The same thing could have happened if I'd been there instead of Sheldon. Though I like to think that it wouldn't have because she was just an old lady, and I would have stepped in as soon as she pushed the preacher down, but whatever. I've got tacos. And I won't have to do her autopsy because it's a conflict of interest, so there's that too."

"Always look to the positive," Jack said, taking the bag of food from me and getting out of the truck.

I looked down the front of my shirt, and there was shredded cheese and lettuce that had fallen from the taco. I reached down and ate some of the cheese before shaking the rest to the ground.

"Always look to the positive," I repeated.

CHAPTER THIRTEEN

Jack used the back entrance and coded himself in through the door, holding it open for me. There was nothing I could do about the issue with the Lichners. It's why we had insurance out the wazoo, though technically the city owned the cemetery, so this was probably going to become their issue to deal with.

Cole was waiting in the office for us when we arrived and he said, "I hope you've got extra in there. I'm starving."

Jack took two tacos out of the bag and then tossed the bag to Cole. "Help yourself. Thanks for overseeing the team for the Downey case."

"You can't be two places at one time," he said, falling back on the couch and digging into the food. "We've had teams out since first light this morning going up both sides of Gambo Creek."

"Find anything?" Jack asked.

"Not until we got to Hangman's Bridge," he said.

Hangman's Bridge was a wooden pontoon bridge over Gambo Creek in Bloody Mary.

"As you know, that bridge is in pretty rough condition," Cole said.

"Yeah, they're supposed to shut it down next month and repair and modernize it," Jack said.

"But right now a lot of the wood is splintered," Cole said. "Including the handrail. We found this." He dug a plastic evidence bag out of his coat pocket and handed it to Jack. And then Jack passed it to me.

"A piece of her lingerie," I said, holding up the lacy fabric to the light. "Cheney can confirm but it looks like the same pattern."

"Yep, plain as could be on the handrail," Cole said. He'd already finished off his tacos, and I took one more out of the bag before the men devoured the rest of them. "Not only that, we've got scrapings on the ramp from a vehicle and tire tracks."

"She was dumped three days ago," Jack said. "Those could belong to anyone."

"Yeah," Cole said. "But maybe we'll get lucky and get a match from one of your cars."

"I need to check in with Cheney and see how it's coming."

"We're still waiting on the warrant," Cole said. "Judge Wallner still hasn't signed off, so the private residences still haven't been searched. Which means Cheney hasn't even gotten started on the cars yet."

Jack went to the phone on his desk and pressed the intercom button. "Betsy, can you get me Judge Wallner on the phone?"

"I can try," she said. "You've got about a thousand messages out here from other judges and attorneys. And they were all so nice too, threatening to have me fired."

"Ahh," Jack said. "I guess that explains it. You know I make friends everywhere."

She hmmphed and disconnected. Betsy Clement had been Jack's secretary since he'd been elected. She'd also been the secretary for the last eight sheriffs before him. Betsy was about a hundred years old and she knew secrets that she would take to her grave. She had no idea how to use a computer, and there was a fifty percent chance she wouldn't use the phone right, but she was a national treasure and the only way to get

Betsy out of that job was for her to die in her chair.

The intercom buzzed a couple of minutes later and Jack answered.

"Judge Wallner on line one," Betsy said and disconnected.

"What's going on, Judge?" Jack asked.

"I was going to ask you the same question," Judge Wallner said. He didn't sound like he was in the best of moods. Everyone knew he suffered from gout, but he had a generally grumpy disposition even when he was in a good mood.

"I've had attorneys and federal judges calling my home phone since last night," he said. "And on top of that, the staffer of a congressman. All night long. They didn't care that I'm an old man and need my sleep, or that I had an eight o'clock tee time this morning. Something about illegal searches without a warrant, intimidation, assault, and verbal threats."

"Uh-huh," Jack said. "That doesn't answer why I don't have the warrant to search the house of a woman who was stabbed thirteen times and dumped in the river. Or why there's a knife missing from the knife block in the kitchen of our upstanding law clerks who work for federal judges and one whose father is a congressman. Delaying only makes it harder."

"Who said I was delaying," Judge Wallner said. "Didn't you hear me say I had an eight o'clock tee time? I'm signing the warrant now."

There was another grunt just before he disconnected and Jack's lips twitched in amusement.

"Well, I guess we have our warrant," he said. "Cole, tell Cheney to focus on the cars and see if we can match what was found on the bridge. And let her know she can send forensics back out to the house to start going through the rest of it."

"You got it, boss," Cole said, getting up from the couch. "Thanks for the tacos."

"How did he eat those without getting lettuce and cheese down the front of his shirt?" I asked, looking down at the front of my own shirt and the wreckage there. Again.

"Trade secret," Cole said.

"Let's see if Cami's roommates arrived," Jack said. "Want to go make their lives miserable?"

"Yeah, I guess," I said, shaking out my shirt over the trash can. "It's just a bad design. Why would someone invent an open-ended shell? They're just setting us all up for failure."

Jack opened the door to his office and waited for me to pass him before closing it behind him. "The taco makers are setting everyone up for failure? Like, our inability to eat tacos successfully is part of their diabolical plan to take over the world?"

"Maybe," I said. "Stranger things have happened. I'm sure Sheldon could tell us all about them."

"But why would you want to ask?"

"I don't," I said, following him down the corridor toward the conference rooms. "I'm just saying we could ask."

"Kevin is still in lockup," Jack said. "I'll leave him for last. Let him keep a little longer in a holding cell. Thea is scheduled first in conference room A."

The conference room was a comfortable space with a long conference table and eight black leather chairs that surrounded it. There was a screen on one wall and a whiteboard on the other, but they were both blank for the moment.

The blinds were open and we could see Thea through the window, sitting alone at the table. She was already dressed in her work uniform and she kept checking her watch.

Jack knocked on the window before opening the door. "Thea," he said. "Thank you for meeting with us. I know you've got to get to work so we won't take up much of your time."

"Sure," she said, sitting up straight. "I want Cami's killer to be caught."

We took the seats across from her and I took a closer look at the silver rings she wore on each middle finger. The one on her right hand said *Justice* and the one on her left hand said *Truth*.

"Interesting rings," I said.

"A gift from my mother when I graduated law school," she said, looking down at them. "Kevin's dad bought him a hundred and thirty thousand dollar Mercedes. I got rings and six figures in student loan debt."

"We want to get a better understanding of the household dynamics," Jack said, leaning back in his chair.

"Like what?" she asked.

"We know that John owns the house," he said. "Any issues with rent payments being late? Money issues?"

She snorted. "Are you kidding me? John's loaded. Like, seriously loaded. His dad owns some shipyard company that has all the defense contracts. He's worth billions. John is dabbling in being a grown-up. He fancies himself buying up all the property and basically being the overlord over the town, renovating everything as he goes so the peasants are grateful he stepped in. It's all part of his twelve-step plan for ruling the country."

"He wants to run for president?" I asked.

"No," Thea said, rolling her eyes. "The president doesn't rule the country. He just does what he's told. John's goals are bigger than that."

"Why bother with law school? Or getting a clerkship? Why live where you are when he could live in DC?"

"It's kind of a love/hate relationship with his dad," Thea said. "John loves the money, but not the man so much. I guess there was the expectation that John would go to law school and build something from the ground up like his grandfather did with the shipyard. John was supposed to go to Harvard Law School. His dad had everything all set, but then John pulled out and applied at KGU instead. Told his dad that the world didn't want another Harvard graduate, but someone who was relatable to the common people." She rolled her eyes. "So buying buildings in places like this is fulfilling the expectation but also giving his dad a middle finger at the same time. I guess John's mom is from King George, so he's at least got ties here. He used to spend summers here as a kid with his grandmother."

"You know anything about his mother or grandmother?" Jack asked. "Where they lived?"

I knew Jack was thinking about where Cami's body was dumped. The location of Hangman's Bridge wasn't in a location that was well travelled or well known.

"No, sorry," she said. "I don't really know much about his family. He doesn't talk about them, and the only reason I know about his dad is because he starts raging about him whenever he drinks too much."

"Does he drink often?"

"Nah," Thea said. "John's pretty controlled in that regard. Sometimes he and the guys will commiserate about stuff at home over a bottle of something. Kevin is always drinking so it doesn't take much to get him to join in, and Will..."

"Yeah. Will," Jack said, acknowledging without words that he knew about the drug problem.

"Well, anyway," she said. "John's always careful not to get caught in situations that might ruin him down the road. He's always preaching at us about risk and reward, like we don't all have our own careers to worry about."

"How long has Kevin had a drinking problem?" Jack asked.

"Since undergrad," she said. "He'd go to frat parties and binge drink. Had to be taken to the emergency room a couple of times for alcohol poisoning. Crashed his car a couple of times and would've gotten a DWI if his dad hadn't stepped in. I'm surprised he's still in jail. His dad usually makes people's lives miserable where Kevin is involved."

"But you stay with him," I said.

"Kevin is a great guy when he's sober," she said. "And he's smart. Really smart. And he's loaded, but he doesn't really care about that. He's just a little reckless sometimes and he's not always thinking straight when he's drinking. His dad helped us both get the clerkship for Judge Perry. Compared to everyone else, our jobs are a walk in the park. Clerking for Judge Perry isn't as prestigious as clerking for Judges Mitchell or Stevens, but any clerkship looks good on a resume. And Kevin manages to handle the workload and his drinking well enough. And he can put on a good face when we're at events or in public."

"You said you and Kevin were thinking about moving to a new place," Jack said.

"Kevin's dad said he would lease us a place in Dupont Circle," she said. "It's a fun area and it's closer to the courthouse. But doesn't look like that's going to happen now."

"Why's that?" I asked.

"Because the stipulation was that Kevin would stay out of legal trouble for a year and then his dad would rent the property to us. With Kevin and I both making payments we could afford it. Barely. But now that he's sitting in jail it doesn't look like we'll be moving out of the slums after all."

"Doesn't sound like Kevin and Will are good at taking John's advice about risk and reward," Jack said.

Thea snorted derisively and took a drink from the bottle of water in front of her. "The one thing I've learned about attorneys is that they're not good about taking advice about anything. It's no wonder the judicial system is such a wreck. No one really cares if they're upholding the constitution or if victims are getting justice. They care about finding loopholes so they're right, even if that means setting a precedent that could destroy future generations."

"Sounds like you're in the wrong business," I said.

"You're not wrong," Thea said. "I hate it. But I've also got six figures in student loan debt to pay off. I earned my way into that clerkship. No one bought it for me. I might hate it, but I don't see as I have a lot of other options right now."

"John mentioned the two of you had a sexual relationship," Jack said, changing course.

"Did he?" Thea asked, the corner of her mouth quirking in a smile. "I'm surprised he even remembers. That's one of the times he was drunk. We were both still undergrads. It was just one of those stupid things that college kids do because the circumstances were convenient. But I can tell you it wasn't good and it wasn't memorable. In fact, it was so bad I helped myself to the cash in his wallet on the way out of his apartment. It paid for a taxi to get home and also my meal plan that semester, so can't say I'm too sorry about it."

"John insinuated that he broke things off because you wanted something serious," Jack said.

She laughed outright at that. "I'm not surprised he'd say something like that at all. He's a narcissistic jackass."

"He also mentioned he's made the rounds with Toby and Cami, but Cami was his more frequent partner."

"John has been unusually chatty," Thea said, brows raised. "Yeah, he and Toby had a thing for a while during law school. But John's not really relationship material and he's a little dramatic. Toby was just trying to get through school and stay focused. The thing with Cami started some-time last year. Toby and I both warned her not to waste her time. John's got a ten-year plan for career, marriage, and family, and someone like Cami doesn't fit the description." She rolled her eyes again.

"In what way?" Jack asked.

"How can I put it delicately," she said, her sarcasm obvious. "John hooking up with women like Cami and Toby and me...that's what he'd call slumming it. We don't fit the pedigree of the future ruler of the world."

"What do you know about Cami's other sexual partners?" Jack asked.

"What do you mean?" Thea asked.

"I mean who else besides John was she sleeping with? There was evidence in her room that she had company the night she was murdered. And John said he was out at a dinner. So that means someone else was occupying her bed."

Thea shook her head and shrugged. "I don't know what you're talking about. Cami didn't have time for that kind of stuff. John was her hookup when she needed sex."

"What about Will or Kevin? They ever hook up with Cami?"

"No," she said, looking at her watch again.

"I'm going to have to go. I've got to be at work in half an hour and I still have to call a ride. I don't suppose you know when Kevin's car will be released."

"It depends on how cooperative everyone is while we're investigating," Jack said. "The longer it takes us to find answers, the longer it'll take to get you all back home and back to normal. Thanks for your time."

Thea smiled tightly and grabbed her purse.

"Thoughts," Jack said, once she was gone.

"She was lying," I said automatically.

"That goes without saying."

"It caught her off guard when you asked who else Cami was sleeping with," I said. "She knows something. Knows there's another guy."

"Maybe she's protecting someone," Jack said. "Reading between the lines, what did you think of her?"

"She's got some bitterness and jealousy," I said. "Resents the fact that guys like John are handed things on a silver platter and she's had to work her way up from nothing and sling drinks at the same time. But doesn't mind taking advantage of the money when it presents itself."

"Bingo," Jack said. "I think that's the nail on the head. She didn't give a thought to taking all John's money from his wallet—a good amount if it paid her meal plan for a whole semester. Just like it doesn't faze her to use Kevin for his car, a new apartment in a better neighborhood, and a clerkship with Judge Perry. She doesn't really care about Kevin. You could tell by the way they interacted last night. But he's a means to an end, and his dad is a congressman. She's not stupid."

"So you think she's protecting her investment by lying about who else Cami was sleeping with? Why would she do that?"

"Maybe Kevin is who she's protecting," Jack said. "He can't sit on that barstool and watch her work all the time."

I raised my brows at that. "So you're presenting the theory that Kevin has been having an affair with Cami. And Thea knows about it, but she doesn't want to give up what Kevin has to offer. Though now that I say it out loud it would also explain why she puts up with his drinking."

"Thea and Kevin were the last people who saw Cami alive, supposedly," Jack said. "Maybe Kevin tells Thea he's going out to grab some dinner or something and leaves her working. Comes home and hooks up with Cami. Goes back to the bar and sits the rest of the night with Thea until she closes up and they go home."

"Still doesn't leave motive or opportunity for Kevin to be our killer," I said.

"No, but it leaves motive and opportunity for Thea to be the killer."

"Well," I said, blowing out a sigh. "That throws a wrench in things."

Jack called Cole and put him on speaker. "Did we ever get confirmation that Cami went to the courthouse the night she was murdered?"

"She clocked in at 11:02 p.m.," Cole said. "Clocked out seven minutes later."

"Thanks, Cole," Jack said and disconnected. "We've got about fifteen minutes before Toby arrives. I want to look at our timeline again. Something isn't adding up for me."

CHAPTER FOURTEEN

I took a detour on the way back to Jack's office to the breakroom. I looked back and forth between the coffee and the sodas, trying to decide which would give me the biggest boost for the rest of the day. I was asleep on my feet, and we weren't even close to being done.

"You okay, Doc?" Cheney said from behind me.

I turned and looked at her, wondering if I'd actually fallen asleep standing up. "Just trying to decide what my future holds."

"Yeah, I know," she said, slapping a file into my hand. "I could smell your brain burning all the way in forensics. Get a soda and a Snickers from vending. You look like you could use it."

"Thanks," I said, deciding that was as good of an option as any. "What am I holding?"

"Those are your red flecks from the Hargrove case," she said. "Banner-red gloss with an additional coating of red metallic shimmer made by Enora Paint."

"What does that mean?" I asked, swiping my card in the vending machine and choosing a Snickers.

"Enora Paint holds the exclusive contract for high school and collegiate-level football helmets. The flecks you found on your victim came from a football helmet. A King George High School football helmet to be precise."

"That lines up," I said. "Thanks for getting it back so fast."

"Yeah, well, I'm putting in for vacation time next week. I'm about to spend the rest of the afternoon taking apart those cars you brought in."

"Gotta catch a killer," I said, enjoying the crack and fizz of the soda can as I opened it. There was such joy in that sound.

"Don't we always," she said and left.

I finished off my candy bar, tossed the wrapper, and then headed back toward Jack's office. As soon as I came in he narrowed his eyes.

"You had chocolate," he said.

"Bring it down, Sherlock Holmes. I brought you one too." And I tossed him the other candy bar I'd gotten.

"You bought this for yourself for later, didn't you?"

"You've got trust issues," I said. "I bought it for my husband because I love him and he works hard. But I didn't get you a drink because you only drink water anyway."

"Fine," he said. "Then thank you for thinking of me."

"You're welcome," I said primly and lay back on the couch. I *had* bought the candy bar for me to eat later, but I would have gotten one for Jack if I'd thought he'd wanted one. It was rare for him to eat anything that was pure sugar, so I knew he must be asleep on his feet too.

"We've got a match on the paint flecks, by the way," I said. "I saw Cheney in the breakroom. Said it's a match for the football helmets at King George High. There's an exclusive contract with a paint company, so I guess it wasn't hard to ferret it out."

"Good," Jack said. "Now we have two murders and two missing murder weapons."

"Them's the breaks, kid," I said. "What are you doing on the board?"

"Trying to work out the timeline," Jack said.

"Toby said she and Cami ate around eight o'clock and then stayed downstairs and talked for a while. And then Cami supposedly got a text message from someone at work, she went upstairs to shower and change, and then left again around ten. We've not recovered Cami's cell phone, but we'll be able to get a transcript of texts from the phone company. Toby saw Cami leave because she knew she had her purse with her, so she was still downstairs. It's an hour-and-fifteen-minute drive to the courthouse."

"That timing is pretty close to when she clocked in at the courthouse."

"Yeah," he said. "Cami's badge said she left the courthouse at 11:09. She didn't have a vehicle so she had a rideshare. We can assume the guy waited for her and just did a round trip. So that would put her home about twelve thirty."

"About the time John got home from his dinner with Judge Mitchell," I said.

"So from twelve thirty to just before three o'clock when Kevin and Thea see her, she's still alive. And in that two-and-a-half-hour time span, she changes into lingerie, lights some candles, sets a scene for romance. For who?"

"Someone in the house," I said. "There are no other players. Who else would show up that late at night? When Thea and Kevin saw her in the kitchen Thea said Cami was holding one of John's favorite reds."

Jack grunted and I could tell he was thinking. There was a buzz on the intercom and Sergeant Hill's voice came through. "You've got a Toby Wallace waiting for you in interview A. And we got messages from the attorneys of John Tippin and Will Matthews. They've declined to come in for interviews."

"Thanks, Hill," Jack said, looking at me.

"I guess someone has something to hide," I said.

"Maybe," Jack said. "Or maybe they're smarter than their roommates. I wouldn't consent to an interview either. That's the smartest thing to do. But people usually can't help but talk about themselves or other people, and regular people generally want to be cooperative or think that when they're asked to come in for an interview that they're required to, which makes it nice for us. Only they're not required to do anything. But when you're in the thick of things generally the best thing to do is to just shut up."

"You'd make an excellent criminal," I said supportively.

"Of course I would," he said. "But I choose to use my powers for good."

We made our way back to conference room A and I was feeling the sugar rushing through my body. I'd crash hard eventually, but I felt like I could run a marathon or at least a 5K.

Toby looked younger today. Her face was scrubbed free of makeup, and she was in an old pair of gray sweatpants and a black hoodie. Her face looked pale and her hair was pulled back in a ponytail.

"Were you able to find accommodations last night?" Jack asked, laying a file down on the table and taking a seat across from her. I sat next to Jack and watched as Toby glanced at the file.

"I went home," she said. "John said he'd put us all up in a hotel, but my parents live in King George so the deputy dropped me off there. I still have some old clothes and stuff there."

"Tell me about Cami and John's relationship," Jack said.

She flinched slightly, but other than that Toby had herself under rigid control. Gone was the weeping girl from last night. The woman in front of us was angry and defiant, but her self-control was impressive.

"It started sometime last year," she said. "I guess it was just one of those things that happens."

"How'd you find out?" Jack asked.

"Caught them in the kitchen," she said, shrugging. "And then in the laundry room. And the second-floor landing." She crossed her arms over her chest. "They really didn't try to hide it that much."

"John mentioned that the two of you had a sexual relationship," Jack said, his voice steady and soft.

"John would have a sexual relationship with a sandwich," she said. "He likes to give this song and dance about convenience and meeting needs, but I'm pretty sure his needs are the only ones being met. I know he never met mine."

"How long did your relationship with John last?" I asked her.

"Almost two years," she said. "He waited until after we'd graduated law school and been appointed to our clerkships to break things off."

"Did it come as a surprise?" I asked her.

"You could say that. We'd been talking about our futures and marriage. Of course, John has a stupid ten-year plan so I would've had to wait until he was thirty, but he's such a convincing liar I probably would've agreed to it. For a while."

"What changed his mind?"

She scoffed. "What else? His father changed his mind. John doesn't have the capability of making choices on his own. He has minor outbursts and rebellions. Like buying the place we're living in and not going to Harvard. But he would never do anything that would upset the promise of being the heir apparent to that fortune. And marrying beneath his station would be one of those things."

"Because of John's mother?" Jack asked.

Toby looked surprised. "Very good," she said. "Yes, I guess that's a mistake John's father didn't want to see repeated. John's mother is from here. She grew up dirt poor. I guess it was some rags to riches story you hear about, but she was a waitress and he took one look and instantly fell in love. And then twenty years later she took half of everything he had in the divorce and moved back to her hometown."

"How's John's relationship with his mother?"

"Okay, I guess," she said. "I've never met her. But I know he goes and sees her and talks to her on the phone. I think he's embarrassed of her, so he's never brought her around."

"Did you know about Cami's relationship with John?" Jack asked.

"Oh yeah," she said bitterly. "Cami's from Florida, and not like Palm Beach or anything that John would care about. She worked hard and earned her way to where she did today. Like I did."

"But not Thea?" I asked.

Toby rolled her eyes. "Thea is a leech. She'll latch on to whoever can take her the furthest. There's a reason she's the only one of us who hasn't taken the bar yet. She's not as smart as the rest of us, and the only reason she made it through law school and got the clerkship was because of Kevin. She hasn't taken the bar yet because she knows she isn't going to pass. And not passing is not an option when you have a federal judge clerkship."

"Did Cami ever share how things were going with John?"

"Just enough for me to tell her that if her hopes were marriage then to get out while she could," Toby said. "I told her about his ten-year plan and the kind of woman his father would approve of, and she kind of laughed it off and said she wasn't looking for marriage and was just looking for something casual to knock the edge off from time to time."

"But you didn't believe her?" I asked.

"No," she said, shaking her head. "Cami was in love with John. It was easy to see. And John is really good at making you feel like you're the center of his universe, when in reality the center of his universe is him. She'd kind of give this attitude like she could take it or leave it, and her workload helped with that. Judge Stevens is no picnic, but at least she doesn't have to work directly with John on a daily basis."

"You and he both work for Judge Mitchell," Jack said.

"I work. John runs around having drinks and dinner and then shows up to take the credit."

"Did Cami and John sleeping together make things difficult with the living arrangements? All of you got along well?"

"We're adults," she said, shrugging a shoulder. "You do what you have to do to get through. But there was definitely tension."

"Between John and Cami?" Jack asked.

Toby sighed and seemed to soften a bit, looking down at her hands. "I told you Cami was in love with John. You just can't hide something like that, even though she was pretending otherwise. And I guess a few weeks ago Cami overheard John talking to his father. He was going to bring Cami to some big company event as his date, and his father had a fit. Called Cami trailer trash and not worthy enough to breathe the same air as John."

"Sounds like a great guy," Jack said sarcastically, making Toby laugh.

"He is most definitely not," she said. "I guess John's dad told him to bang her if he needed to, but to keep his eye on the prize. I guess John's father had someone else in mind to be John's date for the event, and he agreed. Cami didn't tell John she'd overheard, but something in her changed. I could see it. She didn't stop sleeping with him or going out when she felt like it, but she kind of got this jaded edge about her. I think John noticed it too because he started sending her gifts and flowers and being more attentive."

"Did Cami start sleeping with someone else? Maybe out of revenge?" Jack asked.

Toby glanced off to the corner of the room and said, "I don't know what you're talking about."

"Cami is dead, Toby," Jack said. "Why would you protect her killer if you know something?"

"I don't know anything," she said. "Except that I know how the world works. People like John and Kevin and Will—the world is their oyster. They were brought into privilege and they'll never know anything else. There is no work or scraping yourself up from the bottom. They get and they get and they get, and they're never told no. Rules don't apply to them and consequences don't apply to them. You'll see. You think you're smug because Kevin is sitting behind bars? Men like Kevin's dad are smart and they're ruthless. He'll make sure you never win another reelection. He'll come after your property or your family. You can't win against men like that, and there's no point in even trying."

"All that tells me is you don't know anything about me," Jack said, smiling and passing me the file that was on the table, signaling that it was my turn.

I opened the file and started pulling out pictures. Lining them up in front of Toby.

"This is a picture of a knife that came from your kitchen," I told her. "Murder weapon." Though I didn't bother to tell her it wasn't the actual murder weapon.

"That knife from your kitchen was stabbed into your friend thirteen times," I said, putting another picture in front of her of Cami's torso. "You know what kind of rage and anger it takes to do that to another person? Strangers don't do that to people. Someone who knew her held that knife and stabbed it into her over and over again while looking her in the face and watching the life go out of her. Who do you know who could do something like that?"

Toby made a small squeak but her eyes were glued to the picture of Cami's body.

"But it doesn't stop there," I said, pushing harder. "After she's stabbed, someone picks her up and throws her over the side of a bridge and into the water, hoping she'll be carried down fast enough with the rain to end up in the Potomac. That's smart. Because the Potomac is a different state. It'd be out of our jurisdiction. Someone might have found her washed up, or she never could have been found. That's what the killer was hoping.

"It turns out all that rage and the knife wounds in her chest isn't what killed her though," I said, laying out another photo of Cami on my autopsy table. It had the effect I wanted it to because Toby went dead white. "What do you think Cami was feeling? Just the initial assault. That first cut of the knife. And then for it to happen again and again, knowing you were about to die, but still alive to feel the pain. And then you feel that cold splash from being tossed into the water. You don't have the strength to swim or keep your head up, but you try because survival instincts are strong. But then eventually you stop trying and the water fills your lungs and you drown."

"Stop," she said, shaking her head and closing her eyes.

"One of your roommates did that to her," Jack said. "Can you really go back and live in that place knowing that? I'd be wondering which of you is next. Because it gets easier every time you do it. And like you said, guys like that believe they're invincible."

"I don't know," she said, shaking her head as a tear rolled down her cheek. "I don't know who killed her."

"But you know who else she was sleeping with," Jack said. "Who was it?"

"Kevin," she said. "She was doing it to get back at John and Kevin knew it. But he didn't care. I think he's getting tired of Thea and figured if she found out about it maybe she'd break things off with him. So the arrangement bene-fitted both of them."

"She told you all this?" Jack asked.

She sighed and rubbed the back of her neck and then she gave a half-hearted laugh. "Again, I caught them. I'm forever walking in on people having sex. Lucky me. I actually caught them at work. There's a small copy room on the fourth floor, but no one ever uses it because the copier is old and takes forever. But all of the other ones were in use, so I ran upstairs to use it because I was in a hurry. And I walked in on them. Not something that can easily be erased from the mind, believe me. So I closed the door and left them at it, not sure if I should stand guard or pretend like nothing ever happened.

"But the funny thing is that room is right next

to Judge Mitchell's chambers. I guess John was in there with him kissing ass or doing whatever it is he does on a day-to-day basis—he certainly wasn't making copies—but John comes out of Judge Mitchell's chambers with a big grin on his face and I wanted nothing more in that moment than to reach over and open that door. But I think that's why Cami picked that room. She wanted to get as close to under John's nose as she possibly could. Risk makes for exhilarating sex, right?"

"John never found out?" I asked.

"I don't know," she said. "Not that day. I just turned around and walked away."

CHAPTER FIFTEEN

"Now what?" I asked, after Toby left the conference room.

"We'll talk to Kevin and see what he's got to say," Jack said. "See if we can place him as the mystery lover on the night of her murder."

"Why do you think you haven't heard from Kevin's dad yet?" I asked.

"Oh, I've heard from him," Jack said. "I've just chosen to ignore him. There's nothing he can do for now and he knows it. Assaulting an officer is a felony battery charge, and he can't even get a magistrate to set bail until sometime on Monday."

"Are you going to stick with that charge?"

"Depends," Jack said. "My first priority is the

girl who was murdered and finding out who killed her. If Kevin is guilty of murder then felony battery is the least of his worries. If he's innocent and he can help us find who did kill her I'm willing to downgrade the charges to pure stupidity. But nothing and no one is going to get in the way of finding out who killed Cami Downey."

I agreed with him. These people were playing games where there could be no winners. A woman was dead. Brutally murdered. And the people who shared a home with her were keeping secrets, lying, trying to make themselves look good, blaming others, and making it harder for the truth to come out. But the truth could always be found within the lies. It was just asking the right questions and listening for unspoken answers to reveal themselves.

"Since we've got Kevin in jail, I want to look at his hands," I said.

"What for?" Jack asked.

"Because Cami had contusions along her jawline. It was a perimortem injury. A punch to the jaw like that would knock someone out, especially someone Cami's size and weight. It would give the killer the opportunity to get her into the car and drive her to Hangman's Bridge."

"Let's go," Jack said. "We're getting close with this one. I want to check in with Cole and see if anything has turned up with the search warrant. I want John and Will in here. All of these guys will start throwing one another to the wolves for self-preservation. One of them knows something. We just have to get them in here to tell us what it is."

Jack called Cole and set the phone on the table so it could be put on speaker.

"Sheriff," Cole said. "Did you know that you and me and every cop in this county is going to lose his job soon?"

"Oh really?" Jack asked. "That's news to me."

"I figured it would be," Cole said, his drawl lazy. "I've got all kinds of lawyers and some guy named Clark Tippin out here pacing around our crime scene. Media started showing up, I'm guessing because the guy in the fancy suit called them."

"How'd that go over?"

"We moved the perimeter back and are taking our sweet time," Cole said. "And it started raining again, so now they're all wet, so that's lifted my spirits quite a bit."

"At least you're having a good time during your last days as a sworn officer," Jack said sarcastically. "Enjoy them while you can. Have you found a serrated knife hidden under anyone's mattress, by chance?"

"Not a knife," Cole said. "But we found an ounce of cocaine, paraphernalia, and three thousand dollars in cash in Will Matthews's nightstand drawer."

"Oh perfect," Jack said, grinning. "We were just talking about how to get Will and John in for questioning. They politely declined my request."

"So would I," Cole said. "Can't say I blame them."

"I'll send a couple of uniforms to arrest him," Jack said. "Happy hunting."

"Good timing," I said, standing up to stretch.

"I told you we were getting close," he said. "I can feel it in my gut."

"Maybe you just need another candy bar," I said. "I'm switching to coffee before we talk to Kevin. You should bring him some. He's probably got a pounding headache. Maybe it'll make him more agreeable."

"Or we could just torture him with the smell of yours," Jack said. "You should drink water."

"If water tasted like coffee I would drink it," I said. "Besides, there's water *in* coffee."

"I hope you gave your patients better medical advice than you give yourself," he said, opening the door for me.

"That's why I don't work with the living

anymore," I said. "I don't have to feel the burden of preaching what I don't practice."

"How about a compromise? Coffee now and water at dinner."

"Agreed," I said. "And people say marriage is hard. Look at us winning."

I understood the psychology of meeting with Kevin in lockup. There was something about hearing the bars clank shut behind you that made you appreciate freedom a little more, and I knew Jack didn't want Kevin to get comfortable in an interrogation room. Some people needed the sight of the bars as a reminder of what was at stake.

I'd have preferred the interrogation room.

I brought my coffee to my mouth but didn't drink. I was just using it to cover the smell—steel, cement, sweat, vomit—all topped with a thin layer of bleach. My shoes scraped across the concrete floors and I waited for the corrections officer to unlock the door that led into the holding area. Jack had left his weapon in the safe with the guard.

The holding cell area wasn't a large space. There were four gray cells, each with double bunks bolted to the wall and a single toilet. The holding cells were for short-term guests or those waiting to be transferred over to the prison. After the chaos of the night before, I expected all the cells to be full, but we passed only one other man who was lying on his bunk and staring at the ceiling on the way down to the fourth cellblock.

Kevin lay on his bunk, curled on his side with his back turned toward us.

"Time to rise, Sleeping Beauty," Jack said. We waited for the deputy to open the cell and we stepped inside. I wasn't going to sit anywhere, and I was going to have to scour the bottoms of my shoes when we left. That says a lot for someone who embalms people for a living.

"Go away," Kevin groaned. "Let me die in peace."

"No time for that," Jack said. "We're closing in on Cami Downey's murderer. I need you to sit up for me so Dr. Graves can look at your hands."

Kevin rolled so he was sitting on the side of the bed, but his head was hanging down. I could already see the marks on his knuckles.

"Crap," I said, letting out a sigh.

Kevin looked up and I winced at the sight of his face. His left eye was almost completely swollen shut and he had some very colorful marks on his face. The knuckles on both his hands were bloodied and bruised.

"Looks like you had an exciting night," Jack said, eyeing him up and down. "You need a medic?"

"Someone already came," Kevin said. "Hasn't done much good."

"Not much you can do for a punch to the face," Jack said. "It'll feel better in a couple of days."

"Why do you want to see my hands?" Kevin asked, flexing his sore knuckles.

I went over to him and picked up his right hand, feeling around to see if there were any bone chips or broken fingers.

"You haven't been in many fights, huh?" I asked.

"What makes you say that?"

"Your thumb is broken. That's a rookie mistake. Never tuck your thumb in your fist."

"We don't get into a lot of fistfights at the courthouse," he said sullenly. "God, my head is pounding. Why am I the only one still here?"

"I'm still here, mate," the guy a few cells over said.

"Ugh," Kevin said, pressing his fingers to his temples. "Why haven't I been bailed out?"

"Because it's Saturday," Jack said. "And there's

no bond schedule for felony battery of a police officer. You should know better than that. It'll be Monday at the earliest before you can get bond."

"You know it won't stick," he said. "My father will eat you for lunch."

"Uh-huh," Jack said, leaning against the bars and crossing his arms over his chest. "Felony battery might be the least of your problems. A murder charge isn't going to look good for someone like your father. Wonder what he'll do about that?"

"You're not sticking me with a murder charge," he said. "I didn't kill anyone. Especially not Cami."

"Because you were sexually involved with her?" Jack asked.

Kevin looked surprised but pressed his lips together.

"In my experience, a sexual relationship gone bad is a pretty good motive for murder. Especially when the victim was stabbed thirteen times. Did you look at her in the eyes when you stabbed her? What's it like to go from her bed to dumping her body in the creek? She wasn't dead, by the way, when you pushed her over the edge of the bridge. Cause of death was drowning. That's a pretty horrible way to die, isn't it?"

"Stop it," he said, pressing his head harder. "I didn't kill her. I don't want to think about her."

"Someone killed her, Kevin. Someone you live with. Have shared drinks and laughs with. Someone punched her in the jaw and knocked her out and then put her body in the car and drove her to Hangman's Bridge. We're looking at your car right now, Kevin. What are we going to find?"

"Nothing," he said. "God, make the pounding stop. My head is exploding. I didn't do anything to Cami."

"Did you have sex with her on the night she died?"

"I don't want to talk about it," he said, his breath catching on a sob.

"It's not a secret if other people know about it," Jack said.

"Toby," Kevin said. "She walked in on us."

"You think she's the only one? You don't think women know when their man is sleeping around?"

Kevin paled slightly, making the grotesque bruises on his face more vibrant.

"You think John didn't know?" Jack asked. "He was sleeping with Cami too. Were things getting too hard to juggle?"

"She wasn't sleeping with John," he said. "Not

for weeks. Not since she overheard that conversation with his dad."

"He said he was with her Monday night," Jack said. "Maybe she was playing both of you."

Kevin shook his head. "I'm not taking the rap for this. I didn't kill her. And John wasn't with her Monday night. That was me. I was with her. Thea was working so I told her I was heading out to get some dinner. No one was home except for Will and he was probably too busy doing lines in the bathroom to know that I'd even come back. I went back to the bar after and got drunk. It's the only way to not think about Thea, Cami, my life, or my dad. It's best to just keep things as a nice blur."

"You're on the fast track to killing yourself," I told him.

"Well, there are worse things than death," he said, blowing out a breath. "You've not met my father."

"If you didn't kill her then you need to help me out," Jack said. "Because you've got means, motive, and opportunity. You just admitted that you've left the bar to go hook up with Cami, and that it's a regular pattern. That puts reasonable doubt into your alibi for Tuesday night. Thea can't watch you her entire shift. It'd be easy enough for you to slip out."

"I told you Cami was alive when Thea and I got home," he said. "She was in the kitchen. And then we went upstairs."

"Uh-huh," Jack said. "Do you and Thea share a space or do you still have your own apartments? Because it looked to me like you still have your own."

"I went upstairs and went to bed," he said. "My own bed. Thea's apartment is a trash heap. I never sleep there. Sometimes she sleeps at my place. But we both like our own space."

"You weren't curious as to why Cami was downstairs picking out a bottle of wine? Who she was going upstairs to share it with? I mean, it was John's favorite red. Was she picking it out for him? Or did she pick his favorite wine to give him another jab for treating her badly? Maybe the two of you decided to meet up again after you got home. Thea goes to bed and is none the wiser. And you sneak upstairs to be with Cami."

"Please get me some aspirin," Kevin said. "This is torture."

"I'll get you some," Jack said. "Tell us what happened that night, Kevin. Tell us all of it. I can make the felony battery charge go away. I can get you out of here and connect you with a great rehab center. Totally private. No one would even know you're there or be able to find you there. Not even your father."

"Like I said, you don't know my father."

"Sure I do," Jack said. "I know a thousand guys just like him. My name has some weight to it. I can give you my word that you can check in and do what's best for your health. Maybe figure out what you want to do with your life before you waste it. We're only given one."

Kevin started to cry—great gasping sobs into his hands.

"I loved her," he finally said. "Cami. Since we were undergrads. She was a sweet girl from a small town and she was way out of her depth. You should have seen her when she first got to KGU. You almost felt sorry for her. I was a couple of years older than she was, but I was trying to figure some stuff out so we graduated at the same time. Applied to law school at the same time. Just like the other guys.

"But she never paid me any attention in that way. She was always so focused on school. And then John kind of moved in out of nowhere and swept her off her feet. I hated him for that because I knew he didn't really care about her. But you've met John. Not many people can say no to him."

"When did your affair start with her?" Jack asked softly.

"A couple of months ago," he said. "Like I told you, Cami overheard John and his father having a conversation and that kind of did it for her. She said John didn't bother to defend her. He just agreed with his father that she was no better than a piece of trash and told him he'd take some woman named Cici Monroe to the event. Cami was pretty devastated. But being clerk to a federal judge toughens your skin real fast, and you start thinking outside the box. Cami decided what John needed most was a little of his own medicine. That's when she came to me."

"She just presented a proposition?" Jack asked, arching a brow.

"Yeah, pretty much," he said. "I was insulted at first. Kind of pissed too. Here's this girl that I've wanted for forever and she's offering herself to me just so she can get back at her boyfriend. I wasn't flattered."

"I can see why," Jack said commiseratively.

"Then she told me about the conversation between John and his father. And then she just kind of leaned forward and kissed me. That was all it took. I would have done anything she'd asked from that point on."

Jack tapped on the bars to get the deputy's

attention. "Hey, Rook," he said. "Bring me a black coffee and four aspirin."

I heard Kevin whimper in relief.

"She was wild and reckless," Kevin said. "She wanted John to catch us. I didn't care if Thea caught us. It was a dream and a nightmare all at the same time. But then things started to change a few weeks ago. She wasn't as angry, and she told John she had too much to focus on to be his booty call whenever he had an itch to scratch. I don't think he liked that very much, because that's pretty much what she'd been to him and he was used to the convenience. We started stealing these moments together, you know what I mean? We'd schedule time to meet up somewhere for dinner where we knew no one would see us. I'd skip out on Thea at the bar. Cami would meet me during her lunch break at the townhouse my father owns on Dupont Circle.

"Thea tells people that's where she and I were going to move, but that's not true. I'd already asked Cami if she wanted to move there with me. Both of us get away from all the drama here and kind of start over in our own space."

"Anyone know about that arrangement?" Jack asked.

"No," he said. "We didn't tell anyone. We thought no one even knew about our relationship except Toby. But like I told you, Cami was wild and reckless at the beginning. It could have just as easily been John walking in on us in that copy room rather than Toby. I was almost sick to my stomach afterward, thinking Toby had told John or maybe he'd heard us. The one thing John hates most in life is to lose. He didn't want Cami, but he sure as hell wouldn't have wanted to lose her to me."

"Would it have made him mad enough to kill her?" Jack asked.

"No...I don't know," he said. "Listen, I can't imagine anyone killing her. We've all known each other for a long time. Everyone has their quirks and vices, but I wouldn't say anyone had the capability to kill anyone."

"I guess it just depends on the reason," Jack said.

The guard came back with the coffee and aspirin, and Kevin looked up hopefully.

"What really happened the morning Cami died?" Jack asked.

Kevin sighed and closed the eye that wasn't swollen shut. Jack walked over and handed him the coffee and aspirin, and Kevin muttered, "Thanks," as he took them. And then he looked up at Jack. "I'm sorry I punched you."

"I appreciate it," Jack said. "But I'm not sorry

you're in here. This is a good wake-up call. We'll help you if you let us."

"Maybe," he said, knocking back the aspirin and wincing as the hot coffee touched his tongue.

"Tell me about the morning Cami died," Jack repeated.

Kevin sat back on his bunk and pulled his knees up, wrapping his arms around them. "It was like you said. I went to the bar with Thea like usual. The only reason I go is because she gives me free drinks. My dad watches my bank statements and I'm not supposed to be in bars anymore."

"Thea seems to think your relationship is pretty serious," Jack said.

"Thea is an opportunist," he said. "I know that. I've just never cared. She's just trying to get a leg up in the world, you know. She grew up in poverty, so she's coming at it from a different angle. And the sex was pretty great, so I wasn't going to rock the boat. It's not like I was going to marry her. And as far as I know she didn't want to marry me either. And weirdly enough, my parents like her okay. But I think my dad sees everything from a political standpoint. Like it's a good thing I'm hanging out with someone who grew up like Thea did."

"You drink too much Tuesday night?" Jack asked.

"No," Kevin answered. "Hardly anything. Told her I wasn't feeling that great. Thea mentioned maybe I'd caught whatever it was Cami had. Cami had stayed home from work that morning." Kevin cleared his throat and looked down. "That was one of our scheduled days. Cami stayed home from work and pretended to be sick and I had a bunch of research to do that day, so everyone thought I was holed away somewhere. I just brought all my work home and she and I spent the day together. It was nice."

He was lost in his own thoughts for a couple of minutes and then took another sip of coffee.

"Thea got home from the library around four," he said. "She had to be at work at six, so it was easy for me to leave the house before she got home and then come home again like I'd been at the courthouse all day. I changed clothes and drove her to work. I told her I had some work to catch up on, which I did because I hardly got anything done all day, so I walked across the street to the all-day-breakfast place. I came back about nine o'clock. It wasn't super busy, so I sat at my usual place at the end of the bar and watched the baseball game and ESPN after that until it was time for her to close.

"I'd texted Cami to let her know I was on the way home," Kevin said. "That's why she was in the kitchen getting the wine. She knew I was on the way. It was like Thea said. She was wearing that dumb fluffy robe she loves and holding up a bottle of two-hundred-dollar wine. Thea asked if I wanted her to stay the night with me, but I told her I really wasn't feeling well and just wanted to go to sleep. Told her I thought I'd caught a stomach bug or something. She seemed fine with that and went to her room. If you stand at the right spot on the third-floor landing, you can see down to our floor. So Cami texted me about twenty minutes later and said the coast was clear."

"We never found her phone," Jack said.

"She never went anywhere without it," Kevin said. "None of us do. Our lifelines are tied to those judges. On call twenty-four seven." He finished off the coffee and crushed the cup in his hand. "When I went upstairs she had all these candles lit. Wine and glasses. Very romantic. And she wasn't wearing the ugly robe anymore."

He cleared his throat.

"We decided that we couldn't keep sneaking around anymore," he said. "We were all adults and none of us were married. There was no point keeping on with stolen moments and secret messages. We knew Thea would probably be hurt, and who knows what John is ever really feeling, but I already had plans to move out and into the city anyway, so this just sped up the timeline a little. I didn't figure everyone would still be fine living together. You can only pass each other around so much before things just get weird.

"I mean, John's slept with Cami, Thea, and Toby, but he's never been able to keep it in his pants. Got busted for paying a prostitute and having a fake ID when he was in high school, but his dad got all that fixed. I've slept with Thea and Cami. Will has slept with Thea and Toby. I'm too old for all that crap now. Life is already complicated enough."

"Did you go back down to your apartment?" Jack asked.

Kevin shook his head. "No. I stayed the night. I had to be up for work at six. After we, uh, finished, you know, I fell asleep. Cami kind of woke me up and said she was going to clean up and take a shower. I'm not sure what she did after that because I just grunted and went back to sleep.

"I had my alarm set, and when I woke up she was gone. I figured she got up early or maybe never went to sleep to get caught up on work. So

I went back to my place, showered and got ready for work. And then I took Thea and Toby to work that morning. Will rode with John. Toby said she hadn't seen Cami, but then she told us about how she'd had to go in late last night to pick up some files, so we all figured she took a rideshare and went in early."

"It didn't worry you when you didn't hear from her?" Jack asked.

"Oh, it did," he said. "But I figured maybe she'd changed her mind or got scared off about moving in together and telling everyone about us. And then the longer she was gone the more pissed I became. So then I just started getting drunk again. I'd mostly stopped drinking when Cami and I were together. I knew she didn't like it, and I didn't like not being in control when I was with her. She made me want to be better."

Jack stood up straight and moved away from the bars, signaling for the deputy to let him know we were wrapping up.

"Who's got access to your car?" Jack asked him.

Kevin looked surprised at the question. "Everyone I guess if they wanted to. There's a table downstairs right when you walk in. That's where keys and mail go."

"I hope you're playing everything straight

with me, Kevin," Jack said. We left the cell and the bars closed behind us.

"I am," he said.

We were a few steps down the corridor when Kevin asked, "Did you mean it about rehab?"

"Every word," Jack said. "I'll start making some calls."

CHAPTER SIXTEEN

"I want to go look at the body again," I told Jack once we were back in his office. "We need something concrete to pin on one of these guys."

"They're bringing Will in on the cocaine charges, so I'm going to stay and talk to him," Jack said. "I've not heard back from Joe Able. If we get this wrapped up early enough maybe we can stop by there and close both of these cases tonight."

"Even better if we could do it before dinner," I said.

"It's after four. We'll make a judgment call. I know your candy bar is starting to wear off."

"Don't worry," I said, leaning up to kiss him on the cheek. "I'm going to get another one on the way out."

"Eat something green when you get to the funeral home," he said as I waved goodbye. It was nice to have someone who worried and took care of me.

My fingers tapped impatiently on the steering wheel. I was anxious to get back to the funeral home.

The parking lot was blessedly empty, and I tried to put out of my mind the disaster from the funeral earlier in the day. The truth was, Mrs. Lichner had made poor decisions in her grief and it had cost her life. Other people's decisions weren't something any of us could control. I knew our safety protocols had been in place for an open grave in the cemetery. We'd roped off the area and covered the hole. But unfortunately, we lived in a society where people thought it made sense to sue someone for their own stupidity. The city would probably end up having to settle with the family. And hopefully Mrs. Lichner's funeral would be held at the Here and Now Funeral Home over in King George.

I keyed myself in the side entrance and locked the door behind me. I'd forgotten to get my candy bar from the vending machine in my hurry to look at Cami's body again, so I figured I didn't need to eat anything green to counteract it.

I let myself in the lab and took the stairs

quickly, my footsteps echoing on the metal steps. I didn't turn on music like I normally did. I went straight to the refrigeration unit and rolled Cami's body out on the gurney and over to my table. Once I got her lifted onto the table, I started the initial process of the autopsy again.

I turned my lights on high and pulled them low over the body, so I could see every hair and fiber on her skin. I looked for bruises or puncture marks I might have missed that I'd thought had been caused by debris from the creek. But there was nothing except for the bruising along her jaw.

The bruising was visible on her skin, but that was understandable considering that area of the face isn't a deep tissue area. It is a sensitive area and a person wouldn't need a lot of force if they knew where to hit to knock a person incapacitated. Because the bruising had already been at the surface, I hadn't looked any deeper. I'd measured the bruise and notated it in her chart. And the size and spread of the bruising was large enough for a man's hand.

I went to my tool cabinet and got out a device that looked like a large flashlight. It was an alternate light source and it worked perfectly for seeing things beneath the surface. I wanted to take a closer look at that bruise.

"And there you are," I said less than five minutes later.

I set up the light, took new measurements, and took several photographs to add to the file. Jack called just as I was cleaning up and getting ready to text him.

"Just heard back from Cheney," Jack said. "She found strands of hair in the trunk of Kevin's car. And a very small trace amount of blood. Kevin's car was just as clean as John's. Apparently John had hired a detail company to take care of both vehicles."

"Convenient timing," I said.

"Apparently someone made the suggestion and John decided it was a good idea," Jack said. "Will was very talkative once we started talking about prison and finding enough cocaine and cash in his drawer to charge him with distribution."

"Well, I found something on my end too," I said. "Come pick me up. I'm ready to put this thing to bed."

We were silent as we made our way back to King George Proper. The windshield wipers swished rhythmically and water that had collected at the side of the road splashed up into a wave across the sidewalks.

"Maybe we're not meant to have kids," I said out of the blue. It was something that had been on my heart that I'd been too afraid to say out loud. My fists were knotted in my lap, waiting to hear what Jack would say.

I could see him glance at me out of my periphery and he was silent while he thought things through. That's one of the many reasons Jack was good at what he did. The words he spoke were always well thought and had purpose.

"Maybe we're not," he said. "But that's a bridge we'll cross when we get to it. Right now the desire of our hearts is to start a family. And I believe that desire will come to fruition. Maybe the waiting is a lesson in patience. Or maybe the waiting is because we're supposed to practice on a dog first."

"I like the dog answer much better than practicing patience," I said.

"I figured you would," he said. "I love you. You know that, right?"

"Yeah," I said, squeezing his hand. "I know that."

"You heard from Lily?" Jack asked.

"I texted her and asked if she and Cole wanted to have dinner tomorrow night," I said.

"Sneaky," Jack said. "She answer back?"

"She said she'd let me know and then wished us happy hunting. And she let me know she'd be attending the Walling funeral tomorrow with Sheldon to make sure there were no catastrophes. Apparently the Lichner funeral will make the second page in the *King George Gazette* for the Sunday paper."

"Free advertisement for the funeral home," Jack said, grinning.

"Shut up," I said, mouth twitching.

Even this early on a Saturday it was impossible to find parking in front of the Mad King. The rain was apparently driving everyone crazy, and no one wanted to be stuck in their homes anymore.

Jack found a space where he could pull up on the sidewalk again, and he flipped on his lights. The two units behind him positioned themselves so the street was partially blocked.

We walked into the bar and scanned over curious faces. And then we saw Thea behind the bar, serving a customer and laughing at something they said. She looked up and caught sight of us and her smile faded. She knew why we were there. I could see it in her face.

People moved out of the way as we walked toward her, and those sitting on the stools at the bar scattered, taking their drinks with them.

"You guys here for a drink?" Thea said, her smile back in place.

"I need you to take your rings off and put them in here," Jack said, holding out an evidence bag.

"I don't think so," she said. "These are important to me. Like I told you before, a gift from my mother."

"The warrant covers anything in your personal residence or on your person," Jack said. "You really don't have a choice."

She stared at Jack for a few seconds and then one by one took the silver rings off and put them in the evidence bag.

"I need to see your right hand," I told her.

She turned to me and I could see the wheels turning in her head, trying to figure out the best angle to play this out. She finally handed me her right hand. I knew just where to touch. Thea gasped and pulled her hand back, cradling it in her other hand.

"The jawbone is hard, isn't it," I said. "No tissue there to soften the blow of impact with your knuckles. And then with your ring...you probably chipped a bone. That's why your hand is still so sore."

"I don't know what you're talking about," she said.

"Sure you do," Jack said. "You killed Cami Downey."

A deputy came up behind the bar and started reading Thea her rights.

"You're grasping at straws," she said. "You'll never prove it."

"Tip for the future," I told her. "Don't wear a ring when you punch someone. It leaves an impression in the tissue. Easy to match once you know what to look for. I can line your fist up directly with the photographs. Perfect match."

"You knew about the affair between Cami and Kevin," Jack said. "And you knew your good luck days were coming to an end. A woman knows these things, right? You knew or suspected something was off. Maybe that they were meeting at the Dupont Circle house. Or maybe that Kevin was going to ask Cami to move in with him instead of you. But you kept on pushing and claiming your territory.

"You really started to get nervous when Kevin stopped drinking so much," Jack said. "That's when you knew something was wrong. You kept giving him drinks and he either didn't drink them or nursed them all night. It was easier to control him when he was drinking. So when you came home from work and you saw Cami in the kitchen getting wine, did you know she was setting the scene upstairs for Kevin to join her?"

Red streaks of color appeared on Thea's cheeks and anger flashed in her eyes.

"Kevin snuck upstairs and spent the night with Cami," Jack continued. "They talked it over and they were going to stop hiding their affair. There was no reason to keep dragging things out with you or John. They wanted to live their own lives. Your friends don't think very highly of you. One called you a leech and another an opportunist."

Thea stayed silent, but her anger intensified to the point I was surprised she didn't explode with the rage she was holding inside. I could see now how easy it would have been for her to stab Cami so many times. Once you were that filled with rage anything was possible.

"How'd you find out for sure?" Jack asked. "Did you go back to Kevin's place? Maybe under the pretense that you were just checking on him to see how he was feeling. You had access to his apartment. But he wasn't there. There was only one place he could be. And that's when you started planning.

"Cami came back downstairs to the kitchen and that's where you were waiting for her," Jack said. "If you'd argued much you would have woken up the whole house. So what'd you do? Probably just sucker punched her as soon as you saw her. She would have been wearing her big robe, but you took it off her. It probably made it too cumbersome to get her to the car.

"You had access to Kevin's car as well. Keys on the table. All you had to do was get her to the garage and into the trunk. It's hard moving a body, isn't it? But Cami was small and she probably wasn't knocked out long. You had to get her in the trunk. They found her blood and hair in the trunk, by the way."

"It's Kevin's car," she said, shrugging. "That doesn't prove I did it."

"That's for the lawyers to figure out," Jack said. "But with the evidence we have and you basically signing your name on Cami's face when you punched her, we're pretty confident in making the arrest for murder.

"Clever of you though to suggest to John that he should use his car guys to detail both vehicles. Will told us that was your suggestion. You're good at manipulating circumstances, aren't you. You grew up poor so you figured manipulating other people was the easiest way to get where you were going. I'm sure a psychologist would have a field day with you."

The deputy pulled Thea's hands behind her back and put the cuffs on her. The bar was completely silent—even the TVs had been muted —as everyone watched what was unfolding.

"John went along with your suggestion and had both cars detailed while you were all at work. But blood is really hard to remove. Here's what I think happened. You shoved Cami in the trunk and by the time you got to Hangman's Bridge she was awake.

"We did a little background on you, by the way. At first we thought maybe John's mother and grandmother had lived in that part of town. Hangman's Bridge isn't well known, and it's not easy to get to. But you grew up just a couple of miles from there. Your dad worked for one of the nearby farms."

"Yeah, and the farm went under," she said. "Dad left to find work and Mom was left with three kids living in a shack. So what?"

"The water was high when you got to the bridge and you scraped the bottom of the car as you drove onto it. We leave evidence every-where we go. It's almost impossible to be untraceable. You left marks on the bridge, marks on the car...hair and blood in the trunk.

That's where you stabbed her the first time, isn't it?" Jack asked.

Thea jerked against the deputy holding her, her eyes narrowing at Jack.

"She was awake when you got to the bridge. You could probably hear her screaming or pounding against the trunk. You already knew you were going to kill her. That's why you took the knife from the kitchen block. Stupid move, by the way. That immediately made us start looking at the five of you closer.

"You knew the only way to get her quiet and pliable was to make your move as soon as you opened the trunk. You didn't want to fight. Fighting leaves marks." He held up the bag with her rings in it. "So you opened the trunk and stabbed her in the chest. Dr. Graves can show you all the knife wounds and point out which was the first blow. It was a shallow stab wound and didn't hit anything but flesh and rib, so not a lot of blood. But it was enough to surprise her and allow you to get her out of the car. Your rage had taken over by that point. Stabs to the abdomen and chest. She couldn't fight back. She was just trying to protect herself. And it made you angrier because she was still wearing the lingerie she used to seduce your boyfriend.

"Thirteen times you stabbed her," Jack said.

"And then you tossed her over the railing and into the water. The lingerie snagged on one of the beams. And then you tossed the knife in the water with her. Got back in the car and drove home. You took Cami's robe to your room until you could hang it back in her closet. Did you really think you wouldn't get caught?"

She shrugged and her smile was pure evil. "I heard you myself. Cami died by drowning. Looks like nobody murdered that bitch except for Mother Nature."

"Take her away," Jack said to the deputy.

CHAPTER SEVENTEEN

THERE WAS STILL A COUPLE OF HOURS OF DAYLIGHT left once we'd gotten back in the truck. It was dinnertime, but we still had loose ends to tie up. I wanted to get it done, pick up Chinese food, and take it home where I didn't have to see anyone else but Jack for the next twenty-four hours.

"Good catch on the rings," Jack said.

"Yeah, well, maybe with enough evidence a jury won't care about her Mother Nature defense and will lock her up where she belongs. What about Kevin?"

"I connected him with a rehab facility my family helps support," he said. "I made him a deal that I'd drop all the charges if he'd check himself in and stay there. I'll check in with him in a few days and see how he's doing."

"You can't save everyone," I said, putting my hand on his arm.

"No, but if you see a glimmer of hope in someone then you have to try. But they've got to do the work."

"What about the Ables?" I asked.

"That is a place where there's no hope," Jack said. "Look at my phone. I got an email from forensics after they went back to the Hargroves' and looked for more prints."

"They found viable prints beneath the chair," I said, reading the report quickly. "But no match yet on who they belong to."

"Which is why we're going to see Joe Able, whether he's ready for us to talk to him or not. I had Martinez reach out and make an appointment with him at home. He's expecting us. Maybe we should go on a date."

"Right now?" I asked. "Seems inappropriate during a murder investigation."

Jack rolled his eyes. "I meant later. Dinner out. Someplace nice."

"I was thinking sex, followed by Chinese food in bed and a *Peaky Blinders* marathon," I said.

"I like your idea better," he said.

"So what's the plan here?" I asked. "How do we match fingerprints with the ones on the chair?"

"Martinez and Riley will meet us there," Jack said. "We've got a warrant to fingerprint the entire household since they all have immediate access to the Hargroves'. It'll help eliminate all of the other fingerprints found in the study as well. And I've got a warrant to search for the clothes he was wearing that morning. Even if he was ducked down under the desk there would still be blood spatter somewhere. Most likely on his shoes."

"It's sad, really," I said. "Cami Downey and Coach Hargrove. Killed because they were a stumbling block for other people. Greedy people. What kind of world do we live in where we've resorted to wanting something so badly for ourselves that we're willing to take another human life for it if they get in the way?"

Martinez and Riley were already parked in front of the Hargroves' house and Jack flipped on his lights and then back off again as we passed them to park at the Ables' home.

Joe Able was standing in the front door, waiting for us as we walked up the porch steps. And then he watched as two other units parked in front of the house.

"What's all this about?" Joe said, taking the papers Jack handed him.

"It's a warrant to search the premises," Jack

told him. "Is there somewhere we can talk privately? I'm sure Mrs. Hargrove has been through enough."

"She left a couple of hours ago to go to her daughter's," Joe said, reading the warrant. "I don't understand. Why are you looking through our clothes? And for a football helmet? I've got lots of football helmets. I played semi-pro ball. We've got a basement full."

"Let's go inside," Jack said again.

"Sure," Joe said, standing aside so Martinez and Riley could file through and then four more deputies I didn't know by name, only by sight.

"We can go in the kitchen," he said.

"What in the world is going on, Joe?" Ada asked, storming into the hallway, drying her hands on a cup towel. "They're going through our things."

"They've got a warrant," Joe told her.

"So call our attorney," she said. "This is ridiculous. Thank God Lydia isn't here to see this."

"Let's go in the kitchen," Jack said. "Is your son home? We need to keep everyone contained while the search is going on."

"No," Ada said. "He's having dinner at a friend's house tonight." And then she turned angrily on her heels and went back into the kitchen.

"Sorry," Joe said. "She's been really upset by all of this. She and Lydia are close like sisters, but things have been strained."

"Since she found out what Steve planned to do with the team for the upcoming season?" Jack asked.

Joe stopped and looked at Jack. "Yeah, I guess you'd know all about that stuff by now. Come on back. Y'all want coffee or anything? I've already got a pot made."

"I'll take some," I told him. "Just black is fine."

"Sheriff?" Joe asked.

"None for me, thanks," Jack said. "I'll be up all night."

I gave Jack a curious look. Joe Able was not acting like a man who had anything to hide.

Ada was putting away food from dinner and stacking dishes precisely in the dishwasher after she rinsed them off.

"Why are there cops going through my home?" she asked again. "I don't care about a warrant. If you've got a warrant it means you believe we're hiding something or that we had something to do with this."

"Ada likes to watch crime shows," Joe said with a small smile.

"This is serious, Joe," she said, scowling at him.

"I'm not sure Lydia told you, but Steve Hargrove's death has been ruled a homicide," Jack said.

Ada stopped stacking dishes and stared at me. "That's a cruel thing to do to Lydia," she scolded. "I can understand why you'd want to make Steve's death easier on her by telling her it was murder, but she told me how she found him. He blew his head off. There was no one else here."

"Come sit down, Ada," Joe said. "I'm sure they wouldn't call it a homicide if they weren't sure."

Ada dried her hands on a cup towel again and came to sit by her husband.

Jack looked at Joe steadily, biding his time. "Who else could have done it but you, Joe?" Jack asked.

Ada gasped and was poised to stand up but Joe put his hand on her arm and held her down.

"Ahh," Joe said. "So this is what this is about. You think I killed Steve."

"Joe would never hurt anyone," Ada spat angrily. "He's the best man I know."

"They would have heard about the argument Steve and I had a couple of weeks ago," Joe said. "We were all upset when we found out what the plans were for the team and the football program. So to answer your question, Sheriff, I can think of a lot of people who could have killed him."

"Everyone else has an alibi," Jack said. "Your son had left for school. Your wife for work. The team and coaches were all accounted for at the weight room. Lydia was at the grocery store. But you were here at home. Alone. You know where Steve keeps his shotgun. And you know the back door is unlocked. All you had to do was walk over and confront him before he left for work."

"Except I didn't," Joe said. "I told you I heard the shotgun blast. I just figured he was at it with the squirrels again. I was barely up and hadn't even started getting ready for the day. I don't usually go into the office until ten on Fridays."

"Stop talking, Joe," Ada said, patting his hand. "We need to call our lawyer. Don't say anything else."

"I didn't do anything," Joe insisted, looking at her with hurt in his eyes. "Surely you don't think I did."

"Of course not," she said. "But we should call our lawyer all the same."

"You can do that," Jack said. "We can make it formal instead of informal. Those are your rights." And then Jack started reading Joe his Miranda Rights.

"I don't believe this," Ada said, putting her arm around Joe. "This is wrong. You're wrong."

"We've also got a warrant to fingerprint everyone in the house," Jack said. "There are so many prints in Steve's office it'll help us narrow it down."

Joe laughed. "Don't kid a kidder. You found prints on the weapon or somewhere and you're trying to find out who they belong to. I'm happy to give my prints. Because I'm telling you I didn't do it."

Jack nodded and called for Riley to come in.

"If you didn't do it, we'll eliminate you and keep looking for the real killer," Jack said. "It's all part of the process."

Joe let Riley take each of his fingers and press it against the ink pad before placing them on the white index card that was already labeled with Joe's name and personal information.

"Can I wash my hands?" Joe asked Jack.

"In the kitchen sink," Jack said.

And then Riley turned to do the same to Ada and she crossed her arms over her chest and leaned back in the chair.

"I don't see why I have to do this," she said. "I won't do it. I want to speak to an attorney first."

"That's not how this works, Ada," Jack told her. "We have a warrant for your fingerprints. And your son's for that matter. We can either get them willingly from you now or we can take you in and do it formally at the police station."

"Then you can do it formally," she said, stubbornly.

"Ada," Joe said sternly. "That's enough. Just let them take your prints. You've got nothing to hide and you're just delaying the officers' investigation. They're trying to find out who killed Steve."

"They think it's *you*," she yelled at him.

"Well, it's not. So I don't care. Just give them your prints."

Big tears welled in her eyes then, and a sob caught in her throat. She looked at Joe again and she said, "I can't. I can't let them take my prints."

Joe came back to the table and sat down, but he never took his eyes off his wife. "Why can't you, Ada?"

Another sob caught in her throat. "I didn't mean to," she said, grabbing on to Joe's arm. "I was just going over to talk to him. To make him see reason."

"Ada," Joe said, appalled, scooting his chair back.

I was completely taken aback. And I could

tell Jack was thrown off a bit too. This was not the outcome I'd expected when we came here.

"The best thing you can do is tell the truth," Jack said. "I know it doesn't seem like it. You want to protect yourself. But the truth always comes out. We do have prints. On the underside of Steve's chair. You see the killer knew about things like blood spatter and blowback from a weapon. So they put Steve in the chair and pulled it toward them so they could position the gun in his hand and so the spray wouldn't get all over them."

She sobbed again and crossed her arms over her chest. And then she looked at Joe.

"He's my baby," she said. "Derek is my baby and Steve was going to ruin his entire future because he couldn't let go. Endorsements, scholarships, a chance to go pro. All of those things gone because of Steve."

"Steve was trying to help Derek," Joe said, shaking his head. "I didn't see that at first. It was too easy for anger to take over. But he was trying to help all those boys become better men. The worst thing to happen to that team and Derek was Archie Hill. We haven't had control of Derek since that man came to town."

"He's our son," she said forcefully. "And I would do anything for him."

"That's where we differ, Ada," Joe said sadly. "I don't know what to tell you. But you'll never justify killing a man—a good man—for your son."

Martinez came in with a pair of white shoes in a clear evidence bag. "Luminol picked up traces of blood in the treads and in the fabric of the laces."

"Where'd you put the helmet, Ada?" Jack asked.

She stared at the shoes and then looked down at her lap. "Tossed it into the creek behind the house," she said. "I was going to go down there and bury it, but there have been too many cops next door and the rain has been too bad. I was afraid I'd get stuck down there and have to call for help."

"You should probably call that lawyer now," Jack said to a stunned Joe.

Joe nodded numbly and watched as Ada was put in cuffs and led out of the kitchen.

"I'm sorry," Jack told him. And then we left a shattered man alone in his kitchen.

"This has been the longest weekend of my life," I told Jack after we'd left the Able residence.

"And it's not even over yet," he said. "If my calculations are correct, we still have sex, Chinese food, and a *Peaky Blinders* marathon ahead of us. And church, a funeral, and pre-marriage counseling with Lily and Cole tomorrow."

"The job of a cop never stops," I said. "But maybe don't call it pre-marriage counseling in front of Lily. We don't want to scare her off."

"If I managed to talk you into marriage, I'm sure we can get to the bottom of Lily's reluctance. But you're right. The job never stops. It's a good thing I've got a great partner to keep me company."

EPILOGUE

Two weeks later...

The waiting was the hardest part.

Somehow, waiting with Jack didn't make it any easier. But I'd promised him I would tell him whenever I was going to take a pregnancy test, and I was good for my word. Because if I wasn't good for my word, this is the time I would go back on it.

The experts say it's best to take the test first thing in the morning. I was at the point where I would try anything, so I got up, took the test, and then put it on the back of the toilet and left the bathroom as quickly as possible.

I pulled on a pair of sweatpants and an old KGU T-shirt and followed the smell of coffee down two flights of stairs. It was supposed to be my day off, but I was too wound up. And if the test was negative the last thing I wanted to do was stay home and mope all day. So I was rearranging things in my schedule in my head, and ultimately decided to get caught up on paperwork and inventory for the funeral home.

Jack looked up from the stove as soon as I walked into the kitchen. He was making breakfast and spooning eggs and bacon onto plates. I could see the nerves in his eyes, which was somehow comforting because Jack never got nervous about anything. He raised his brows at me in question.

"I left it upstairs," I said. "We're supposed to wait three minutes."

He rolled his eyes. "Has it been three minutes?"

"Probably," I said, tugging at the hem of my shirt.

"Come on," he said. "We'll go up together. And then we'll come down and have breakfast. Maybe we can catch a movie this afternoon."

"I thought you were going in today," I said.

"I can do what I want," he said, pulling me by the hand back up the stairs. "I'm the sheriff."

"You're also bossy."

"That's what makes me a good sheriff."

I followed him back into our bedroom, only

slightly dragging my feet. And then I just decided to get it over with. Me delaying it wouldn't change the result on the test, so I took a deep breath and marched into the bathroom. I grabbed the stick without looking at it and went back to Jack.

Now was the moment of truth. Was I pregnant? I wanted to be. But I knew better than most that we didn't always get what we wanted.

I looked down at the test. Then I looked at Jack.

"Well?" he asked.

Dear Readers,

I'm excited to introduce you to town of Laurel Valley and the O'Hara Family! Here's an excerpt of **Tribulation Pass** and you can look for two more Laurel Valley novels coming in 2024! Check out my website for release dates.

Love,
Liliana

Hattie knew she'd found it the second she crested over the hill.

It sat like a perfect jewel nestled between rolling hills, the white clapboard buildings lined up like soldiers and the streets paved with brick. She could see for miles, past the town and across fields as green as emeralds, with white fences and horses dotting the landscape. A lake rippled like liquid glass and was framed by the majesty of white-capped mountains.

She'd left the top down on her Mini Cooper despite the threat of a storm. The wind whipped through her hair, leaving it unruly and tangled, but she didn't care. The sky was gray with clouds that hung low and swirled overhead. If it hadn't been so unladylike she would've let out a battle cry that would have put the rumbling thunder to shame.

For the first time in her life, she knew what it felt like to be free. There was no one to tell her where to go or what to do, how to sit, stand, walk, or make small talk. There was no one to tell her where to volunteer, what career path to take, or how many children she should have.

Freedom.

She breathed in deep and let the fresh air settle in her lungs. For the rest of her life, she wanted to remember this feeling—everything about it—from the smell in the air to the taste of the first raindrop on her tongue.

Bags and boxes filled every available space in the tiny car. Derek would have a fit at the thought of her driving something so undignified, and her mother would have agreed with him, but Hattie had planned her escape for the last two years, down to the last detail, and she'd thought the little car was impractical and cute—two things she'd had very little of in her life.

Atticus Cameron had helped her get her new identification, and with that, she'd been able to open her own bank account. It was the first one she'd ever had that had only her name on it. Derek had made sure she added his name to the trust her father had left her. She hadn't had a choice. It was never worth the fight that ensued when she disagreed with him. Besides, her mother had felt having Derek control over the money was the best option as well. Margaret Ashbury had been infuriated when her husband's fortune had gone to Hattie. With Derek in control, she could still get her hands on it through him.

For the last two years Hattie had lived in numbness. Living wasn't even the right word. She was a zombie. Her pride always got her in trouble. And she wasn't one to flinch when a hand was raised in her direction. But that wasn't

Derek's favorite form of abuse, though he wasn't above using physical force to get his way.

What he really enjoyed was the psychological warfare, tearing away her self-esteem and security. Calling her names or telling her she was stupid. If she displeased him he'd freeze her out or cut her down in front of her mother or his friends or co-workers. Or he'd make sure she knew when he visited his mistress and come to her at night with the scent of another woman's perfume still on his body.

She'd taken Atticus's advice, squirreling away the allowance Derek put in her account every month and tacking Visa gift cards onto her grocery bills so it didn't look suspicious. He never looked beyond what was put on the debit card, as long as it was spent where she'd told him she was shopping. It had taken patience and perseverance, but finally she'd made her escape.

Atticus and her father had been close friends, and they'd worked together on occasion. The day they stood over her father's coffin was the day he made her promise to come to him for anything, no matter how big, if she was ever in need. She owed him more than she could ever repay, and Atticus had wanted to do a heck of a lot more than provide her with the means for a new life. He'd wanted to put a fist through Derek's face, but Derek moved in some powerful circles, and she didn't want anything to ever happen to Atticus or his family.

She'd scrimped and saved over those two years, and found the secondhand car in excellent condition at a roadside dealership in Connecticut. Atticus had let her keep it in the garage of his Manhattan offices until she was ready to leave for good.

And then fate had lent a hand, and Derek had left for a prolonged business trip to Europe. Hattie had given him her itinerary before he left so he knew where she'd be, and then on a foggy morning on the way to a ladies' luncheon, Harriet "Hattie" Ashbury had died when her car missed the curve in the road.

Again, Atticus had helped her with the logistics of it all. He'd taken care of the scene, the body, and the medical examiner's report. And by the time Derek had flown back from London, she'd been zigzagging her way through the country, checking media reports and newspaper clippings to make sure everything had gone according to plan. She'd become Hattie Jones. And Hattie Jones wasn't a high-profile attorney's wife. She was a wilderness woman with a taste for the great outdoors. And she was free.

She could only imagine what her father

would have said if he were still alive. He'd have wanted to know how she'd gotten into this mess. She wouldn't have had an answer for him. Derek had been charming and sweet, and he'd swooped in to comfort her when she'd been grieving. She'd thought he'd been the man of her dreams, but instead he'd become her nightmare.

Her father...God, she missed him. Some days the grief reached out and grabbed her by the throat until she couldn't breathe.

Atticus had given her a second chance, and by God, she wasn't going to waste it. He'd given her a home to lease and a place to work. And with luck, she could settle in and make friends, become a part of something.

The contents of the boxes rattled as she drove over the uneven surface of the road. She looked down at her phone, but it was no use. No service. She was going to have to stop for directions.

Welcome to Laurel Valley.

There was a neat white sign with those words printed in block letters and a planter box beneath that was overflowing with purple and yellow flowers. The town was even better than Atticus had described.

She knew she was coming in at the end of high season. Atticus had told her the population of Laurel Valley was only a couple thousand during the off-season, which was spring and fall. But during the summer and winter the population could grow up to forty thousand people. The fewer people she had to be around the better. At least for now.

It was one of the most beautiful resort towns she'd ever seen, and she'd seen a lot of them. The architecture was Bavarian, and the chalet-style businesses made up the downtown area of Laurel Valley. Flowers rioted everywhere—out of planters and pots—the brilliant colors standing out against the white of all the buildings. The main tourist streets made a large plus sign, and in the middle of the plus sign was a seating area with tables and umbrellas where people could sit with their coffee or eat lunch. Atticus had told her in the winter it was converted to an ice-skating rink.

There were boutique hotels and tasteful condos that blended right into the mountainous landscape, but the downtown area was surprisingly empty. Only a smattering of cars lined the main strip. Obviously, people had enough sense to stay in out of the upcoming weather.

She slowed the car and read the signs that hung above each of the doors—florist, bookshop, ice-cream shop, bakery, feed store, mercantile, photography studio, and several boutiques she was going to have to check out later. She watched as shopkeepers turned over their open signs to closed and locked the doors.

Hattie looked at the darkening sky again and her grip tightened on the steering wheel as the wind whipped across the open top of her car. People must think she was insane. She pressed the button to raise the top on the car and checked her GPS again. She couldn't be too far from the house she'd leased from Atticus. He told her she'd have as much space and privacy as she wanted, and views she'd never see anywhere else in the world. It sounded like heaven.

The rumbles of thunder were still in the distance, but the storm was moving quickly. She'd been traveling for two weeks, and now that she was this close to her destination, she couldn't wait any longer to get there.

Her goal was to find the house, make a hot cup of tea while the storm rolled in, and then sleep for a couple of days straight. She wasn't scheduled to start her new job as manager of the sporting goods store until next week, so she had time to catch her breath. And maybe over time, she'd learn to stop checking over her shoulder to see who was behind her.

Hattie parked the car in front of the restaurant on the corner, glad to see it was still open. *The Lampstand* was carved into the thick wooden timber over the doorframe. The restaurant was built in the chalet style like the other buildings, but this one was three full stories, though the shutters had been closed over the windows of the top two floors. But at the very peak of the roof was a bright light that was growing ever brighter in the darkness.

Time was of the essence, so she left the car running, struggling to get the car door open. The door slammed shut of its own volition and she ran up the short stairs, wincing as flower petals were ripped from their stems, swirling into the air in front of her.

As soon as she stepped under the wooden overhang she tried to put her hair back into a semblance of order before stepping through the door. Her stomach grumbled as the smell of food assaulted her senses. Between the adrenaline and nerves, she'd mostly been living on caffeine and power bars, with the occasional drive-thru meal tossed in. Getting to Laurel Valley had been the most important thing.

She wasn't exactly sure what time it was, but the sun had been up for a few hours, glaring into her rearview mirror as she headed west. At least until the clouds had started rolling in.

The restaurant was charming. A replica of many of the European chalets she'd seen on her travels. It was the view she noticed first. The entire back of the restaurant was windows that faced the famous Twin Peaks and the lake.

The restaurant felt peaceful—all wood and light and heavenly smells. It was a casual place, open for breakfast, lunch, and dinner, but it was clean and well cared for. Obviously a staple for the locals as there was a section off to the side where several men were playing checkers and drinking coffee, seemingly unbothered by the weather.

There was a group of teenagers in the farthest booth, giggling and completely absorbed in their own world, and in the booth next to theirs was a single man in a deputy's uniform, reading the newspaper and eating his breakfast. He didn't seem to be bothered by the teenagers, or much else for that matter. He barely gave her a glance when she walked inside.

"Welcome to The Lampstand," the girl behind the hostess stand said. Her face was still soft and rounded with youth, and she couldn't have been long out of high school. Her dark hair was piled artfully on top of her head, and she wore a white button-down shirt and a black pleated skirt that came a few inches above the knee.

"Some storm coming in," she said. "You're smart to wait it out until it blows through. You look like you could use some coffee. I'm Mac."

"You're right about the coffee," Hattie said. "But I'll take it to go, please." She smiled cautiously at the girl. She'd been amazed how friendly all the people she'd encountered on her journey had been. She'd lived in a bubble in New York, and most of Derek's associates hadn't been the nicest people.

"You're not from around here, huh?" Mac asked.

"What makes you say that?" Hattie asked.

"You've got a Yankee accent," Mac said. "We get a lot of visitors during season, and we're always trying to figure out where people are from. We're pretty good at it. I hope you didn't come all this way for tourist season. Everything wrapped up last week. Great shoes, by the way. I saw some just like them in *Cosmo*."

Hattie resisted the urge to run out the door and jump back in the car. Just because the girl could place what area of the country she was from didn't mean she was going to get on the phone to Derek and tell him she was alive.

The only person who knew her identity was Atticus Cameron. And it had to stay that way. If Derek knew she was alive he'd come after her with a vengeance, and there was nothing or no one who could stop him.

THE LIES WE TELL

By her calculations, Grace Meredith had exactly five and a half seconds to take out six targets before an alarm sounded. She had a round in the chamber and five in the magazine of her M40A5. Piece of cake.

She ignored the mosquitoes the size of hummingbirds searching for exposed flesh, and she disregarded the sweat that dripped steadily down her spine as she looked through the scope of her rifle. The temperature was in the mid-nineties, but the canopy of trees that blanketed the area held the heat in like an oven and slowly baked anyone who didn't have shelter with a running AC. Her body and mind were disciplined, so the discomforts barely registered.

Colombia wasn't known for its gentle climate.

Or gentle anything for that matter. Gemino Vasquez was Colombia's baddest arms dealer, and lately his biggest client had been North Korea. But Vasquez had something Grace wanted very badly. Something that would bring in a big, fat paycheck from the South Korean government.

She shifted slightly, and the bark of the large tree branch she'd lain on for the last four hours ground against her stomach. But her focus was absolute. Not even the hundred-and-fifty-foot drop to the ground could distract her.

The orange sun blazed just over the tops of the trees, but it would disappear completely in another twenty minutes. By the time it was gone, she'd have the flash drive in hand and already be across the border to Venezuela.

Grace did one final check of all her equipment and took a deep, steadying breath, slowing her heartbeat so her pulse would be in time with-b each shot. She'd hit the sentry at the top of the Vasquez compound first and then take the rest in order from left to right. She pushed her feet against the tree for balance. The clock ticked in the background of her mind as she put the slightest amount of pressure on the trigger.

"One," she whispered. She didn't wait to watch him fall but moved to the next target. Five seconds until the report from her rifle reached their ears. Five seconds for five more kills.

Two...

Three...

Four...

Five...

Six...

Grace didn't stop to check the accuracy of her shots. She never missed a target. She hung her rifle on a tree branch, already missing the feel of it in her hands. Time was of the essence now, and she couldn't afford to be burdened with too much equipment—she'd have to leave it behind. The new guards would be driving up soon for the shift change, and she had to be long gone by then.

She unzipped her supply pack, pulling out a lightweight pipe no longer than her forearm. It looked completely worthless at first glance. In reality, it was a military prototype she'd borrowed from her former life. She hit the button on each end of the pipe and it expanded in length until it was almost as tall as she was, and then she hit the button in the center and waited as wings made out of a synthetic material unfurled to complete the hang glider.

"No time like the present," she said, swallowing as she perched on the edge of the tree and looked out across the jungle. She had a straight shot into the compound, but any shift in wind would have her hurtling into trees. Falling to her death wouldn't bring her the money she needed, so she had no choice but to take a leap of faith. Literally.

Fifteen minutes until all hell breaks loose.

Grace grasped the bar and jumped. The bottom dropped out of her stomach as she free-fell for just a brief moment, and then the air caught beneath the wings and she soared through the treetops like a phantom. It took all her strength and concentration to keep the glider on a straight path to the compound roof, and when her feet touched the ground her muscles were fatigued and her skin coated with perspiration.

She hit another button on the long metal tube and the glider folded itself back up until it was small enough to fit back in her pack.

The body of the first sentry she'd shot lay face down in the greenish-blue water of the swimming pool. A hazy cloud of blood ballooned from under him, and his arms and legs floated like waving ribbons.

Her eyes and ears were alert, but all that greeted her was growing darkness and silence.

Even the animals and birds in the jungle knew something bad was about to go down.

Grace unhooked the harness and pulled her SIG from a thigh holster. She stood silently next to the gray door that led from the roof down a set of stairs to the main floors of the house. Two heartbeats passed before she opened the door and slipped inside. It was quiet, but that wasn't unusual at this time of the day according to her intel—six sentries on duty surrounding the compound, only two guarding Vasquez's private suite of rooms.

Vasquez's stupidity only made her job easier.

Grace walked silently down the thickly carpeted hallway as if she weren't about to steal the schematics for a new superweapon—a weapon that used state-of-the-art laser technology—and sell it to another country. But the closer she got to Vasquez, the more her spine tingled in awareness that something was wrong. That tingle had saved her life more than once, and she never ignored it. The hallway opened up into a landing just as she reached Vasquez's private rooms. Weak light filtered through the windows and cast rainbows as it pierced the glass chandelier that hung overhead.

She saw firsthand exactly why her spine was tingling.

Both sentries were slumped against each other—a dead man's embrace—one with a broken neck and the other with a hunting knife in his carotid. Efficient work considering the size of the sentries.

She pushed the bodies out of her way with her foot and eased the door open, her trigger finger at the ready on her SIG. All that mattered was the flash drive. If she didn't produce it, then she didn't get paid.

She crept into the room. The smells of new death were thick and cloying in the heat, and she could taste the fresh blood in the back of her throat with every breath she took. Dust motes danced in the air, and long shadows were cast in the fading sunlight.

Grace waited for her eyes to adjust and listened for sounds of footsteps, but all she heard was the gentle whir of the wicker fans that rotated slowly on the ceiling. She moved silently, staying close to the wall as she checked his suite.

Vasquez's bedroom was bigger than her whole apartment—the furniture oversized and ornate, the colors garishly red. He was set up for sex. The interesting kind of sex by the looks of things. Restraints and various whips and other tools lined one whole wall, and torn condom packages littered the floor. It looked like Vasquez had a busy day. Too bad his afternoon hadn't turned out so hot.

Gemino Vasquez's body lay spread-eagle on his bed. He was naked, and his eyes were open and unseeing. Two shots to the center of the forehead screamed of a professional hit. He hadn't been dead long. She couldn't stop the bitter disappointment when she saw the flash drive was gone from the chain on his right wrist.

"Hell," she whispered and moved to check the covers of his bed, just to make sure it hadn't come off in the struggle. But she knew in her heart it was long gone. Professionals didn't leave loose ends behind. And this was definitely professional. What ticked her off even more was that whoever did it managed to sneak in right under her nose. He had to have known she was watching through her scope and snuck in through the one blind spot she had at the back of the compound.

The stir of air behind her was the only warning she had before an arm locked around her throat.

"Looking for this?" a deep voice whispered in her ear. He held the flash drive in front of her face.

He pressed close against her back and squeezed his arm tighter around her throat so she had to breathe shallowly through her nose. Grace winced as he pressed his fingers against the pressure points of her wrist, and her pistol fell uselessly to the floor with a dull thunk.

Fear never had a chance to take hold. It was anger that drove Grace. Anger that had kept her alive the last couple of years. And she knew how to wield it. She threw her head back and aimed her heel at his knee simultaneously. He dodged her blows as if he'd been expecting them, but the distraction was enough for him to loosen his grip. She swept her leg and brought him to his knees, reaching down for the knife in her boot. The blade gleamed once in the fading sunlight just before it was knocked out of her hand and across the room.

He outweighed her by close to eighty pounds, and he had a good eight inches on her in height. They grappled and rolled, each one blocking the other's strikes with only seconds to spare. It was a well-choreographed dance.

A familiar dance.

The surprise of recognition took her off guard, and she looked up into laughing blue eyes framed by thick, dark lashes she'd always been jealous of. She had time to register that he'd let his hair grow—a shaggy mane of ink black that curled just over his ears and collar,and a face that was covered in a short, stubbled beard—just before her legs went out from under her. She hit the carpet with a thud. A hard body pressed her into the floor, and he held her wrists captive above her head.

"Hello, darling." His breath whispered against her skin. "You've been practicing. Who's your new sparring partner?"

"Gabe," she said. "What do you want?" She bucked beneath him, annoyed at the familiarity of his weight on her.

"I want you, of course." His lips glanced across her cheek to the corner of her mouth, and she sucked in a breath that brought her body even closer to his. After everything he'd done, he was still the only man who could make her feel less than whole when their bodies weren't fused together. She hated him for it. She hated herself for it.

"Go to hell." She struggled against him, but he shifted his weight to hold her down.

"I've been there, thanks." He cupped his hand against her cheek—gently—softly. "You still feel good against me. Stop wiggling and we'll talk. Don't you want to at least hear my offer? Especially since I did your dirty work for you."

She stilled her body and relaxed, hoping he'd get distracted long enough for her to make a move, and she spoke through gritted teeth. "I don't want anything you have to offer. Just give me the flash drive."

"I figure we have exactly four minutes to get out of this place before the new guards show up for the shift change and Armageddon begins. All I'm asking is that you come back with me and hear me out. If you decide to turn me down, then I'll give you the flash drive with no hard feelings, and you can claim your bounty."

Grace stared at him and tried to decide if he was bluffing. "You know I don't trust you."

"Yes, I believe you've told me that before," he said, his gaze hard. "But what I'm offering will pay more than double any of the jobs you've recently taken. Hear me out."

"Fine." She knew her options were limited. "What are we waiting for?"

"Our rendezvous point is on the other side of the border," he said, rolling off of her. She ignored the hand he reached out to help her up. "We've got twenty minutes to get there or we miss our ride."

Grace had no choice but to follow him out of one hell and into another.

***

The woman hadn't changed a bit in all the years he'd known her. She still kept her deep auburn hair braided tightly down her back while she was working. But he knew what it looked like spread across his pillow, and he knew what it felt like as it slithered like silk across his chest—glorious—a bright flame that was cool to the touch.

He looked at her critically, trying to decipher exactly why he was still attracted to her after the two years they'd spent apart. There wasn't just one thing about her that stood out, but the entire package. Her face was thinner now—her cheek-bones more pronounced—but it was still the face of a sea goddess. Eyes the color of emeralds, slightly tilted at the corners, and full lips that haunted his dreams. She was every desire he'd ever had wrapped in one tiny package.

He let his gaze drift down her body. She was thinner all over. The lush curves he remembered were gone, replaced by a compact body of pure muscle and athleticism. She glanced back at him and raised a brow at where his gaze had landed.

Gabe smiled, but it didn't reach his eyes. He'd been wrong. She'd changed a lot. There was a hardness about her now that hadn't been there before. When she'd first started with the CIA, there had been hope and an ideal of the greater good. Now there was just emptiness—a cold, green stare that didn't believe in anything—and it scared the hell out of him. Because it was no one's fault but his own.

"We've just crossed the border into Venezuela by my calculations," she said, slowing to a jog. "How much farther is your rendezvous point?"

"About another mile. Keep the sound of water to your immediate left." He put his hand on her arm before she could take off again. "Wait."

She stopped dead in her tracks, and Gabe could tell she was trying to hear what he had. They were silent for a few more seconds before the sound came again.

She blew out an annoyed breath. "It's the new guards. You always did have ears like a bat."

"What do you have on you?" he asked.

"My SIG and a hunting knife. How many do you think there are?"

"No more than a dozen. They're noisy bastards. And not too fast." He pulled his own pistol from the small of his back and checked the magazine. "I'll give you a boost." He replaced his weapon in his pants and laced his fingers together. He arched a brow as she looked back at him with irritation.

"I'm really tired of climbing trees." She

exhaled and put her foot into his hands. He launched her up so she could reach the lowest branch, and she swung herself up with ease.

"Do you have good visibility?" Gabe asked.

"Yeah, I see them," she said. "You'll have to draw them close enough so I'm within range."

"Try not to hit me by mistake."

Her grin was sharp as she looked down at him. "Oh, it wouldn't be a mistake."

"That's what I'm afraid of." Gabe left her there to go meet trouble head-on.

He found cover behind a tree trunk the size of a small car and waited patiently. Heavy footsteps crunched over twigs, and he stuck out his foot as two of them passed by. One of the guards tripped and went sprawling to the ground, and Gabe struck out at the other with a palm to the chest, stopping his heart instantly. He broke the neck of the one who was already down before the man could rise off his knees.

Gabe ignored the steady stream of fire that came from behind him—despite her wanting to kill him, he trusted Grace to fight at his side during battle. It was after the battle that worried him.

He went searching for his next victim.

Only a few minutes passed before he stood in the middle of a ring of twelve guards—all of them dead. None of them had fired a shot. She was even better than he remembered.

Grace was waiting for him when he caught up to where he'd left her.

"Time's ticking," he said, looking at his watch.

They picked up the pace and ran the last mile in silence and slowed as they came to a winding dirt road with deeply rutted tire tracks, making footing tricky.

"Did we miss the pickup?" Grace asked.

A forest-green Humvee coated with a thick layer of dust came out of the trees behind them and pulled to a stop. Grace had her weapon out and her finger on the trigger.

"He's mine," Gabe said, opening the back door.

Grace slid across the hot leather seat.

The driver turned and looked at Gabe. Logan Grey had worked with him on other missions. He was a quiet man, tall and sinewy with muscle. He wore his dark-blond hair long, not as a fashion statement, but to help cover the terrible scars on the back of his neck. Logan was former MI6, but an almost fatal accident had gained him retirement before he was ready. Gabe hadn't hesitated at snatching Logan up to join the team. No one knew explosives better than Logan Grey.

"You cut it close, boss," Logan said. "In thirty seconds I wouldn't be here."

"Let's roll," Gabe said. "Be on the lookout for company."

Logan glanced once at Grace and then nodded, putting his submachine gun in his lap.

Gabe closed the window that divided the front and back seat so he and Grace had complete privacy.

"Who's your friend?" Grace asked.

"Logan Grey. Don't worry. He's heard all about you and still agreed to help me find you."

"I'm sure he's a real stand-up guy."

"He'll grow on you," Gabe said, keeping his gaze on the terrain around them, looking for threats. "So what do you think? It's just like old times. We always made a great team."

"Tell me what you want, and then let me go," she said. "I've got a tight schedule to keep."

"You don't have another job lined up once you deliver the flash drive to the South Koreans. Looks like you're a free agent." Gabe watched for a reaction, but she showed no surprise that he'd been keeping up with her movements. She waited him out with her silence and a hard look, and he decided to give in to the unspoken stand-off...just this once.

"I've left the CIA," he told her.

"I heard. Congratulations. Let me go."

Gabe smiled and stretched out across the seat, crowding her with the length of his legs, but she didn't budge an inch. "Did you hear I'd joined the private sector and opened my own agency?"

She laughed, low and sexy, and the smoky sound swirled around him until he was dizzy with desire. "So, good boy Gabriel Brennan has decided to become a bad boy and go rogue. I assume the agency is displeased by your decision?"

"Not at all," he said, shrugging. "They know when something is out of their control. My agency is privately funded and our reputation is above reproach. Even the CIA recognizes the benefits unknown money can buy. Governments are still hampered by rules, for the most part. Sometimes there are jobs where the rules need to be broken. That's when they call me."

"Well, bully for you," she said. "You always did manage to get what you wanted. Everything Gabe Brennan touches turns to gold."

"Nothing could be further from the truth, and you know it," he said quietly. Gabe waited patiently for her to make eye contact. It didn't take her long. She'd never been a coward.

She tilted her chin defiantly. "I don't know

anything about you. I never did. Our life together was a lie. I'm not even sure you know the real you."

He kept his face impassive, even though her words pierced his heart. "How long are you going to pretend she's not sitting here between us?"

"Don't mention her!" The quiver in her voice was quickly controlled. "I'll get out of this car and disappear off the face of the planet. If you want me to stay, then the past stays in the past. It's nonnegotiable."

"Fine," Gabe said. "Whatever you say."

The SUV slowed to a stop, and Gabe pushed the door open, not waiting to see if she'd follow. It was a stupid idea to think he could fix things— to heal the wounds that had been bleeding for the last two years.

Gabe's Gulfstream sat ready for takeoff on the hard-packed dirt the small Venezuelan city called an airport. He went up the stairs and then turned to face Grace, sure she'd still be in the car. But she stood at the bottom of the steps, her face carefully blank.

"You can either come with me or you can leave. The choice is yours," Gabe said without emotion, tossing her the flash drive.

She caught it one-handed and stared at him, studying him, trying to read every angle of the situation as she'd been trained to do at the agency. She finally nodded and started up the steps. "I'll come. A deal is a deal. And my word means something."

Gabe flinched before he could control it and let the pain roll through him. He had a feeling that before this job was over, she'd have one more reason to hate him.

AVAILABLE AT ALL RETAILERS

ACKNOWLEDGMENTS

Getting a book to publication takes an amazing team of people. I'm fortunate to have had these people in my corner for years.

To my editor—Imogen Howson for always making me better.

To my cover designer—Dar Albert for always blowing me away with your talent.

To my children—You're all so special. You have gifts and abilities beyond measure, and I'm excited to see what God has in store for each of you.

To Scott—thank you for answering a ridiculous amount of law enforcement questions and acting out weird scenarios with me. Any mistakes are mine alone.

ABOUT THE AUTHOR

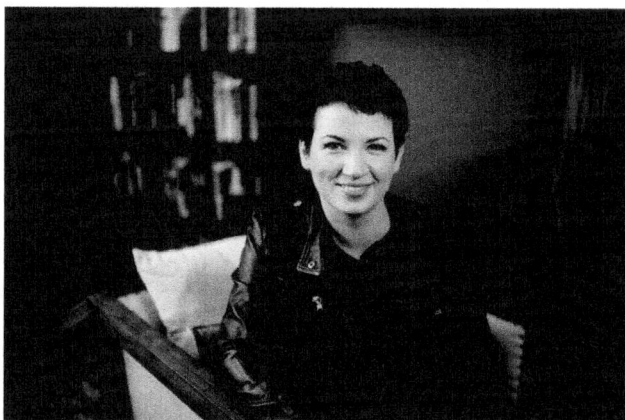

Liliana Hart is a *New York Times*, *USA Today*, and Publisher's Weekly bestselling author of more than eighty titles. After starting her first novel her freshman year of college, she immediately became addicted to writing and knew she'd found what she was meant to do with her life. She has no idea why she majored in music.

Since publishing in June 2011, Liliana has sold more than ten-million books. All three of her series have made multiple appearances on the *New York Times* list.

Liliana can almost always be found at her computer writing, hauling five kids to various activities, or spending time with her husband. She calls Texas home.

If you enjoyed reading this, I would appreciate it if you would help others enjoy this book, too.

Recommend it. Please help other readers find this book by recommending it to friends, readers' groups and discussion boards.

Review it. Please tell other readers why you liked this book by reviewing.

Connect with me online:
www.lilianahart.com

facebook.com/LilianaHart
instagram.com/LilianaHart
bookbub.com/authors/liliana-hart

ALSO BY LILIANA HART

Whiskey on the Rocks

Whiskey Tango Foxtrot

Whiskey and Gunpowder

Whiskey Lullaby

The Scarlet Chronicles

Bouncing Betty

Hand Grenade Helen

Front Line Francis

The Harley and Davidson Mystery Series

The Farmer's Slaughter

A Tisket a Casket

I Saw Mommy Killing Santa Claus

Get Your Murder Running

Deceased and Desist

Malice in Wonderland

Tequila Mockingbird

Gone With the Sin

Grime and Punishment

Blazing Rattles

A Salt and Battery

Curl Up and Dye

First Comes Death Then Comes Marriage

Printed in Great Britain
by Amazon

59584425R00192